THYLACINES

DEBORAH SHELDON

SEVERED PRESS
HOBART TASMANIA

THYLACINES

Copyright © 2017 Deborah Sheldon

WWW.SEVEREDPRESS.COM

ISBN: 978-1-925711-54-7

For Allen and Harry

1

Professor Rosie Giuliani stopped in the doorway. Amazing. The lunchroom was tidy, perhaps for the first time since they had moved into the building some five years ago. Her assembled staff looked like professionals—the techs in new lab coats, the admin suited and booted, not a t-shirt or grubby sneaker in sight, just as she had requested. Rosie smiled despite her nerves. Perhaps today wasn't the beginning of the end, after all.

Beaming, Dr Linda Chang said, "Ooh, I like your haircut."

"Thanks." Self-conscious, Rosie touched her layered bob. "I thought it might help."

Usually, she wore her hair in a ponytail, plait, or bun. Last night, on a panicky whim, she had visited a salon. Image counted right now. *Everything* counted right now. As leader of the team, she couldn't afford to be dismissed by the visiting executives as some doddering old biddy, a grandma who napped in front of the TV. The hairdresser had suggested colour, a shade of ash-blonde, since Rosie's hair wasn't, apparently, the desired platinum or silver but the dreaded salt-and-pepper. She had refused. *I'm sixty-two*, she had retorted, *and I've earned every one of these greys, believe me, through a lifetime of hard work.*

She gazed about at her staff and felt a flutter in the pit of her stomach. Oh no. This haircut had been a mistake. A terrible one. It showed her anxiety, transferred it to them. The techs and admin wore the same frightened expression, were busy catching each other's eyes to share the same message: *We're doomed.*

"Well, what do you think, Professor?" Dr Linda Chang's broad gesture took in the staff. "They scrub up okay, don't they?"

"Oh, you better believe it. I hardly recognised them."

Laughter rippled, but there was a jittery edge to it. Sixteen people, herself included, afraid for their funding. *Shit*.

Pointing at the table, Rosie said, "Fresh cut flowers. In a vase, no less. Nice touch."

Linda nodded and smiled. "My pleasure."

Of course Linda had brought the flowers. She always looked on life's sunny side. But she was wringing her hands, which she never did, and fiddling with her wedding band. And Rosie's staff was always so noisy—talking, joking, whistling, singing. Dedicated and hard-working, yes, but rambunctious. Not now. For Pete's sake, it was quiet as a tomb in here.

"All right," Rosie said, "you pass muster. Take a seat. We still have a bit of time."

She lifted her chin and looked around like a general inspecting the barracks. No photographs, postcards or kids' drawings pinned to the noticeboard any more, no sticky notes on the fridge, the sink clear of mugs and cups, the air smelling like lemon detergent... The lunchroom looked vacant already. Sweet Mary and Joseph.

"Good job," she said. "We'll hold the bulk of the meeting in here. Agreed? We don't want them mucking through our labs. A quick peek at the equipment will suffice."

She halted in front of the pantry and stared at the blank laminate door. The Resurrection Lab's meme poster—a painting of Jesus emerging from the rock tomb with *#JUSTKIDDING* overlaid in big white letters—was gone. As a lapsed Catholic, the poster always made Rosie feel both amused and uncomfortable at the same time, yet she missed it, as if its absence might be a bad omen. She stiffened her spine. How absurd to entertain such a notion.

"Ladies and gents, I'm proud of you," she said, and leaned on the back of her chair, the one at the head of the long table. "First impressions count, and together, we'll make an excellent impression today. I have no doubt about that."

Her staff regarded her with wide eyes. Rosie bit at her bottom lip. If the executives from Clout Energy Drinks Inc. saw all these hangdog faces... No, that just wouldn't do. But how could she raise morale when the entire Resurrection Lab was poised for termination? She was a scientist, not a bloody sports coach.

Linda glanced at her watch. "They'll be here in twenty-nine minutes."

"Fine," Rosie said. "Here's my pep talk, so listen up. As of today, our main sponsor, Dinkum Ales Brewery, belongs to Clout Energy Drinks. Clout has made it clear they will not honour any existing sponsorship deals made by Dinkum Ales without due diligence."

"What a crock," someone muttered.

Everyone began talking.

"Hey, excuse me." Rosie clapped her hands for silence and got it. "Yes, we have an uphill battle. Clout is a North American company with strong links to international sporting events, not Australian animal conservation. At first, they may not see our research as valuable. But we will convince them otherwise." She turned to the window ledge. "Oh. Where are the beer bottles?"

"In the pantry cupboard," said the secretary, a young woman named Indigo.

Rosie opened the pantry. Yes, the bottles were there. Each variety of Dinkum beer had a different Australian species on the label. For the past seven years of sponsorship, Dinkum's limited release—the "Special Edition" porter—had featured the extinct and doglike marsupial, the thylacine, commonly known as the Tasmanian tiger. Ironically, the thylacine was also the star of Tasmania's coat of arms, even though the people of that Australian island had killed off the species by relentless hunting and trapping. In September 1936, the last thylacine had died at Hobart Zoo, not of old age, but neglect. Keepers forgot to put it inside one night, and hypothermia had finished it.

"Perhaps we should put the beer bottles on display again," Rosie mused. "They might tug at the heartstrings, if these corporate bastards have any."

Indigo shrugged and stood up.

"No, wait," Rosie continued. "On second thought, don't show the bottles. It might suggest a lack of allegiance to our new sponsors."

"They're not our sponsors yet," Indigo said. "They might never be."

Especially if they discover how our animals turned out, Rosie thought pensively.

Linda Chang sighed. "I hate to break the news, but a Dinkum conservation program has already had the gong."

"I'm sorry?" Rosie's heart seemed to falter. "What?"

"I got a call a few minutes ago from Burumin Zoo. Their captive breeding program for the southern corroboree frog is over. Clout has pulled funding. Effective immediately."

A collective groan went up. Rosie reached beneath her spectacles to pinch at the bridge of her nose. The southern corroboree frog, about the size of a fingernail, happened to be the poster boy for critically endangered species in Australia. Only about one hundred remained in the wild. And the executives at Clout had tossed the frog onto the scrapheap of history? Already? They had owned Dinkum Ales Brewery for less than twenty-four hours. This was bad. Oh, this was very, very bad.

Everyone was babbling at once.

She held up her hands. "Okay, shush. Calm down. You hear me? Stop."

The room went quiet. Good God, Indigo was dabbing at her eyes with a tissue.

"You're overreacting," Rosie continued. "The Resurrection Lab is not in danger. You know why? Public image. Think of Joe Blow on the street. He doesn't care about a dumb old frog. Why should he? Frogs are cold, they're slimy, they're gross. Let them go extinct, Joe Blow would argue, because he doesn't care. The southern corroboree frog hasn't captured his imagination, right?"

The staff stared at her, expectant, their faces like those of sad and scared children.

Rosie raised a wait-for-it finger and forced a grin. "Aha! But the Tasmanian tiger? A magnificent creature driven to extinction by the folly of mankind? By white Europeans? The same white Europeans, no less, who commandeered Australia? You see the difference?"

"Yeah, sure," Indigo said. "Turn our project into a political hot potato if you want, but it'll backfire. Clout is a multi-billion-dollar business. Their aim is to make money, not right historical wrongs."

"Hang on," said Michael, the newest tech. "Would the average American even *know* about the thylacine?"

"Well, uh…" Rosie rubbed at the back of her neck.

Linda said, "Twenty minutes."

"We're fucked," somebody groaned, and the room erupted into wails and talk.

"Hello!" Rosie shouted, and the hubbub died down. "Listen to me. Yes, Clout Energy Drinks is a North American company. But we're not meeting with Americans. We're meeting with the managing director of the Australian office, Tony Pappas, and his assistant, most likely another Aussie. Remember? They'll know all about the thylacine."

"And care about it?" Michael said. "Like we do?"

Rosie tried to give a hearty laugh. "Oh, who doesn't care about bringing back the thylacine? About de-extincting a whole species? Everybody wants this to happen."

Michael said, "People want the woolly mammoth. Not a weird dog with a pouch like a fucking kangaroo."

The hubbub started up again. Rosie slumped against a bench. Linda approached.

"Can you believe this?" Rosie said. "No one has faith."

"Look, to give you the heads up," Linda said, "I've had an offer from Deakin."

"What?" Rosie said, her face growing hot. "Deakin University?"

"Please try to understand. It's all right for you. You don't have any kids. My eldest daughter is about to start high school. We've chosen a private school, eighteen grand per year. Eighteen grand!"

"But you're head of molecular biology," Rosie said. "*Deakin?* Good God, we compete with Deakin for students. Have you lost your mind? Do you know how this would look?"

Linda offered an apologetic smile and shrugged.

"We're not going to lose this sponsorship," Rosie hissed.

"Maybe not. Just in case, though, have you got a Plan B?"

"Yes," Rosie said, clenching a fist. "We'll go public."

"Public? Oh, no. No! We can't do that—"

"Why not? If we tell the world what we've managed to achieve so far, we'll have donations coming out of our ears."

"But we're not ready for public scrutiny, and you know it. Donations?" Linda rolled her eyes. "No. People will come after us with pitchforks and flaming torches."

Rosie compressed her lips.

Linda had been at her side since the beginning of this adventure some nine years ago. How much flak had they copped from the international science community? Their first year of operation, they had even won the Australian Skeptics Bent Spoon Award for *The Most Ludicrous Science Project of 2008*. Rosie had kept the award, displayed it in her office. A literal bent spoon atop a chunk of wood facetiously described as a piece of Noah's Ark. Sometimes, she gazed upon the award to put fuel back in her tank. *Stuff the haters.* She and Linda had extracted viable DNA from the pickled thylacine pup, hadn't they? And after close to a decade of repeated failures and experimentation, had finally done the impossible: created a living, breathing litter of thylacines, even if the animals were a little… off.

"Hey," Linda said, touching her arm. "You okay?"

Rosie smiled grimly. "We're going to keep our funding."

"Sure, I know." Linda checked her watch. "Fifteen minutes."

Feigning confidence, Rosie winked, strode to the head of the table and clapped her hands to gain everyone's attention.

"One final reminder," she said, "and this is very important: keep it simple. That's what you have to remember above all else. If a Clout executive asks you a question, give him a one-sentence answer. Imagine you're trying to explain our work to a child. Do not, under any circumstances, go into detail. We want to excite the executives, not bore them to tears with scientific mumbo-jumbo they can't possibly understand."

People nodded, murmured agreement.

"And another thing," Rosie added. "Don't tell them anything bad about our thylacines."

"So you want us to lie?" Indigo said.

"Of course not. Just… accentuate the positives." She looked about. "Where's Glenn?"

Linda said, "With the animals, I guess."

***

The door had two signs, one underneath the other:

ANIMAL ENCLOSURE.

DANGER. KEEP OUT. AUTHORISED PERSONNEL ONLY.

Rosie looked through the reinforced porthole window. The enclosure was about the length of two basketball courts placed end to end, with a narrow central corridor. Dinkum Ales Brewery had paid for this purpose-built enclosure, God bless them. The enclosure held three different types of animal. Thirty individual pens lined the left-hand side. Each pen was divided in two by a sliding metal door, which Glenn remotely controlled, to make a front section where the animals were fed, and a rear outside section where they could sun themselves. Along the right-hand side of the enclosure were Glenn's offices, the vet surgery, various supply rooms.

And there was Glenn himself, busy mopping the far end of the corridor. She frowned. Yes, he wore his khaki uniform, but she had expressly requested that he wear long pants today, and he was in shorts, just like bloody usual. She jabbed the code into the keypad. The lock made a clunking sound as it opened, and a buzzer went off.

Glenn looked up, waved, and went back to cleaning the floor.

The door locked automatically behind her. The pungent smell of the animals was a musky mix of ammonia, body heat, dander. Putting her hands on her hips, Rosie stood at the door and waited. Glenn didn't look up. Hell's bells, that man could be so *vexing*. A damn good handler, but he didn't appreciate—or seem to recognise—the chain of command.

"Excuse me," she called, her voice echoing. "Long pants? Did you forget our conversation?"

Glenn leaned on the mop. "Yeah," he shouted. "I did, actually."

"I wanted all of us to look professional."

He laughed. "These knobs aren't going to care about my hairy legs." He propped the mop inside the bucket and ambled down the corridor towards her.

Well, at least the enclosure was clean. Spotless, in fact. Rosie began to walk along the pens, glancing inside at each lone beast.

The Tasmanian devils were eating, their powerful jaws cracking through bones. Their diet was carrion. Glenn had a secret source for rabbit, mouse, and rat carcasses. She had asked him about it once, but he had touched the side of his nose with his forefinger, as if to say, *I'm keeping mum.* She frowned again. There was something so irritatingly child-like about him sometimes. She kept walking. Once Glenn reached her side, he turned and kept pace.

"Good work on the cleaning," she said. "You must have got here early this morning."

"Yeah, about four."

Four? Good Lord. So Glenn was nervous too.

Most of the red kangaroos lounged, dozing. A couple still had their noses in their troughs. Glenn stopped at a pen and made kissing sounds. The kangaroo lifted its head and regarded him with moist brown eyes.

"Hey there, Mabel," he said. "How's my girl today?"

The kangaroo stretched out its neck and put its muzzle close to the bars. Glenn squatted down to rub at the thick, short fur on its nose. Rosie smiled. How could she stay cross at him?

"Mabel had a bit of a temperature yesterday," he said, "but I reckon she's right as rain today. Back on the feed this morning, aren't you? Yeah, too right, my good little girl."

"And the thylacines?"

Glenn paused, gave the kangaroo a final pat, and stood up. "Well, you know..."

"Do they seem any different towards you?"

He shrugged. "Nah, not really."

At two-and-a-half years of age, the thylacines had known Glenn their entire lives. They saw him every day. They relied on him for food. Yet there was no rapport. Curious. The devils and the kangaroos, though not tame in the manner of house pets, were comfortable around him. Quite friendly, in fact. Not so the thylacines.

Rosie and Glenn kept walking.

As they approached the thylacine pens, one of the beasts began to rasp. That must be T1, Rosie thought, the first-born pup who seemed to lead this extraordinary pack. After a few seconds, the five others joined in. It was as if the identical sextuplets were singing. This was not learned behavior. These were the only pups known to exist in more than eighty years. No, it was some kind of ancient, instinctive song buried somewhere in their DNA. The strange wheeze sounded ugly, like a cat's yowl crossed with the sibilant hiss of a snake.

My babies, she thought. *My beautiful, unique, strange babies.*

She stopped at T1's pen and felt the familiar thrill.

The short, sandy-coloured fur and those dark stripes from shoulder to tail… Sometimes Rosie woke at night with the dream of stripes fresh in her mind. T1's head looked like that of a wolf: a long and narrow snout, erect and forward-facing ears, stereoscopic eyes. Yet his body shape and stance brought to mind the hyena, with the tucked-in hindquarters and short back legs. And then his wondrous tail! Unlike any member of the canine species, the tail was an extension of the spine, something akin to the skeletal arrangement of a kangaroo. By God, the thylacine was a remarkable creature. A real-world chimera. No direct genetic relation to any other species for more than eight million years. A biological *marvel*. How on earth could people have been stupid enough to hunt such an incredible species into extinction?

And yet…Were her babies, this precious litter of de-extincted animals, *true* thylacines?

No, she had to admit.

Not really.

The wild thylacine had been about the size of a Labrador retriever. T1 and his brothers were twice that. Why had they turned out as big as Great Danes? Rosie didn't know. Test after test after test, and zero answers. And this was The Resurrection Lab's *second* litter. The first, similarly gargantuan but listless, sickly, mentally impaired, had expired soon after reaching ten months of age for reasons unknown. One morning, Glenn had simply found them all dead. Why? Autopsies gave no explanation.

Oh, she couldn't lose this funding. She just *couldn't*.

"We'll be sweet, Rosie."

She startled, having forgotten for a moment that Glenn was at her side.

"Yes, of course," she said, recovering with a lift of her chin.

The thylacines stopped singing, all at once, as if cut off by the chop of a conductor's baton. T1 sat back on his tail and stood up on hind legs, forelegs dangling, in the manner of a kangaroo. One by one, his brothers did the same.

"How do they know to imitate T1," Rosie said, "when they can't see each other? There's a sheet of metal between each pen."

"Yeah, nah. It's got me buggered."

"Yet you spend all day with them."

"And all night too, sometimes."

"You must have some idea. What's your theory?"

"Language," Glenn said at last. "A kind of secret communication."

"Despite not being taught how to vocalise by a thylacine mother?"

Glenn rubbed at his chin. "Well, I've got a budgie that got took from his parents at five weeks. He's two years old now and behaves like any other male. Courts the mirror in his cage, whistles at it, spews up seed likes he's feeding a young'un. Some stuff is built in."

"Not this," Rosie said. "This is not inherent behaviour. More like telepathy."

"Hah. You believe in that kind of bulldust?"

"No, I don't. But I can't think of any better explanation."

The thylacines, simultaneously dropping onto all fours, approached the bars of their cages. Their moist and dog-like nostrils winked.

Rosie knew they were sniffing her.

Knew they were looking upon her as prey.

It always gave her a creeping sensation of dread within her bowels. And the fixed stare of their large, unblinking eyes. Black eyes, jet black, no distinction between the sclera, iris and pupil, even when the nictitating membrane was retracted.

"Do you ever feel like they would eat you if given the chance?" she said.

Glenn laughed. "Every damn day."

It didn't make sense. Back in the late nineteenth century, when thylacines were still plentiful throughout Tasmania, people used to keep them as pets. Pets! *Gentle and loving*, proclaimed the scientific notes on the extinct species. *Docile.* Another mystery. Exhaustive research into the many deviances apparent in this litter, and not a single answer... *yet.* She needed a little more time to figure out the bugs in the process. God, if she lost the funding...

If she were still a believer, she would ask a saint for a prayer of intercession. As it was, she could do nothing but fret.

At the opposite end of the enclosure, a devil screamed. Agitated, the thylacines yipped, snapping their jaws. And then it hit her. Bloody hell, *why were they so full of beans*?

"You sedated the thylacines, like I instructed," she said. "Didn't you?"

Glenn scraped the toe of his boot against the concrete floor and averted his gaze.

"Please," she said, voice rising. "Tell me you sedated them."

"Hey, you want these tigers snoring on the floor? Dull as dishwater? Yeah, they're feisty buggers, so what? How glorious! Let's show off their true colours."

A flash of panic made her stammer. "Oh no, oh shit. If you give them medication right now, how long until it kicks in?"

"Aw, come on, nobody wants to see a bunch of Tassie tigers asleep. That won't get us the money." Glenn flung out his arms. "Look at these awesome creatures. Just look at 'em!"

Snarling, T1 thrust his front paws through the bars and batted at the air.

The buzzer went off. Rosie jumped, and spun around as the faraway door to the enclosure opened. Linda appeared, her face strained.

Rosie's stomach dropped.

"They're here," Linda yelled.

2

George King, transfixed, stood before the full-length mirror in the manner of a gunslinger about to draw, arms propped out and both hands open. He wiggled his fingers.

"You sure you want to fuck with me?" he whispered. "Okay, mate. You asked for it."

Slowly, he reached around to the small of his back. He had the gun tucked into the waistband of his jeans. The walnut grip felt warm and smooth against his sweating palm. With a flourish, he brought out the .38 Smith & Wesson revolver and held it at hip level.

"*Blam*," he said. "Dead meat, motherfucker."

Smiling, he flexed his arms at the mirror. He looked good. Yeah, the gun suited him. With his shaved head, moustache, full Ned Kelly beard, and beefy frame, he was every inch the total bad-ass. Except...

He sighed. Too bad his t-shirt hung a little too short, revealing the bulge of his gut. But all of his t-shirts had become too short. With his free hand, he hauled up his jeans. As soon as he let go, however, the waistband slid down again. Fuck. He raised both arms overhead and gazed morosely at his hairy belly button. The blue t-shirt had brown, crusty sweat-stains at the pits. Defeated, he dropped his arms. The weight of the gun hit against his thigh.

That's right. *The gun.*

Lifting it again towards the mirror, posing with it, George felt a fresh surge of confidence. Yeah, he looked like a tough guy, for sure, gut or no gut. He bared his teeth.

"You better watch your step," he whispered, "or else you'll be getting—"

The doorbell rang.

Jolted, he almost dropped the revolver. Hastily, he tucked it into the back of his waistband and left his room, closing the door against the unmade bed and the dirty clothes over the floor. He jogged across the lounge. Through the frosted glass panes of the front door, he could make out two figures. He flung open the door.

"G'day, you bastards," he said, "I was just—"

What the fuck?

There was a strange man standing next to Hannah.

"What happened to Davo?" George said. "Who's this prick?"

Hannah smiled. "My friend, Llewellyn."

"Louellen? Isn't that a girl's name?"

"Different spelling, mate, but yeah, it's unisex," Llewellyn said. "Pleased to meet ya."

Flummoxed, George gaped at him. Llewellyn was five foot nothing, raw-boned, and young—about twenty or so, the same age as Hannah. With the dopey eyes and the slow, nodding head of a stoner, he looked about as intimidating as a puppy. Davo, the dim-witted bodybuilder, at least had *presence*.

"I don't understand," George said. "Where's Davo?"

Hannah flicked back her long, ginger hair and shrugged. "He couldn't make it."

"Couldn't make it? We've had this assignment planned for almost a week."

"He got the apprenticeship and they told him to start going to school or whatever."

"Shit." George pulled cigarettes from his jeans pocket and lit one. "This is fucked, Hannah. You should have told me."

"I only found out this morning."

"So where did you find this dickhead?"

Instead of bristling at the insult, Llewellyn snorted out a giggle, which made George even angrier.

"Don't be a meanie," Hannah said. "He's in my Animal Lib group. You remember that blockade of the abattoir when a truck driver ended up in hospital?"

"What about it?" George said.

"That was Llewellyn."

George's eyes bugged. "He was the one that put the truckie in hospital?"

"Nah, not my kind of deal," Llewellyn said. "I'm strictly non-violent."

"But he was there," Hannah said, "and got arrested. And his picture in the paper too."

That's right, George thought with a nasty little flush of envy. He'd recognised that dopey face. From the newspaper, as it turns out. He scowled. Llewellyn smiled and nodded.

"Well?" Hannah had a duffel bag on her shoulder and began to fidget with the strap. "It's cold out here. Aren't you going to let us in?"

Huffing, George stepped back. Llewellyn followed Hannah into the lounge. While she put down the bag, ran her fingers through her long hair and sat down, Llewellyn dropped open his mouth and took in the mahogany furniture, floral lounge suite with dual recliners, blue Wedgewood plates in the buffet cabinet, and laughed.

"Oh, man," he said with shining eyes. "You still live with your parents?"

George slammed the door shut. Mum and his stepfather were both at work, thank Christ. He held the cigarette between thumb and forefinger and sucked hard, exhaling smoke through his nostrils like a dragon.

"Llewellyn, don't bring up stuff like that," Hannah said. "There's no call for it."

"Why not? It's okay by me if a forty-year-old bloke wants to live at home."

Actually, George was forty-two. He straightened to his full height of six feet, approached, put the smoke into the corner of his mouth, and crossed his arms. "I'm a warrior. An anarchist. Every day, I fight the good fight. That takes time and effort. Warriors don't have the luxury of jobs. We're too busy changing the fucking world."

"Yeah, no worries, I get it. Does your mum cook your dinners?"

Every single night. Blushing, George hesitated. "No."

"Shame. I wish I still lived with me old ma. She makes the best food. Like ratatouille. Skinning the capsicums. That's her secret. Char them under the grill and the skins come straight off. She skins the tomatoes too, but I think she puts them in hot water to do that part."

Was Llewellyn taking the piss? George couldn't tell.

"What about your washing? Does she clean your undies?"

"Shut the fuck up," George said.

Llewellyn held up his hands and chuckled. "We're cool, mate. No disrespect."

"My dinners and my laundry are none of your fucking business."

"Sweet. Totally my bad for getting personal. If it makes you feel any better, I take my washing round to Ma's every Sunday. Actually, that's when I get me some ratatouille."

The pulse throbbed in George's temples. He wanted to punch this shithead straight in his gormless face. "So what if you go to your mum's every Sunday? I don't give a shit. And I don't need you to make me feel better about anything."

Llewellyn blinked and smiled. "No worries, mate. Just trying to get past your animosity."

"Oh, stop it, both of you," Hannah said. "All this bickering is giving me a headache."

"He started it," George said.

She said, "Please, Llewellyn, stop pushing his buttons. Remember Occupy Melbourne? George was there, camping out day after day in the City Square, protesting capitalism. Long after most of us had given up and moved on, he was there."

Llewellyn, rocking back and forth on his heels, nodded. "Cool."

But George had never got his picture in the paper.

Llewellyn flopped into a recliner—the one that Mum used, no less—and pulled the lever, swinging out the foot rest. The dopey prick looked so *comfortable*.

"Why are you even here?" George snapped.

"Because I asked for his help," Hannah said. "Don't be silly. We need three people."

George stood over the stranger and said, "Okay, now it's my turn to ask the questions."

"Go for it. I'm an open book, mate."

"What do *you* care about this assignment?"

Lacing his fingers behind his head, Llewellyn said, "I'm a vegan. I haven't eaten meat or animal products since I was eight. I don't wear leather or wool. I don't even have a feather doona. That's why I agreed to help Hannah. Because animals aren't a resource, mate. Not in my eyes. They ought to be free to live out their lives in peace, in the wild, where they belong." He raked his cool, green eyes up and down George, and added, "You like to protest. I get it. The excitement, the adrenaline: it's a rush. And you want to stick it to The Man. Yeah, I get that too. We've gotta break the system down before we can build something better for everyone." He smiled, but this time it wasn't too friendly. "Now, let me ask you the same thing you asked me. What's *your* reason for taking on this 'assignment'?"

George blinked. "Are you for real?"

"Oh, come on, guys…" Hannah whined.

"You've got the balls to sit in my Mum's fucking chair and give me the third degree?"

Fingers still laced behind his head, Llewellyn shrugged.

George crushed the cigarette into his stepfather's ashtray. Panting with anger, with humiliation, he pulled out the Smith & Wesson. Hannah's eyes widened.

Llewelyn, however, only chortled and shook his head.

"You sure you want to fuck with me?" George whispered.

Hannah leapt up. "Guys, please, we've got animals to save."

"I won't be disrespected. Not by this little shithead. Not by anyone."

"Put that gun away," she said. "Now. Right now."

With a glare at Llewellyn, he tucked the revolver into the waistband at the small of his back. Hannah nodded her approval.

"Llewelyn, apologise," she demanded.

The bastard got out of the recliner. "Yeah, look, I'm sorry, mate. I didn't mean to rub you the wrong way. No disrespect intended. I know you've got a good heart."

He put out his hand. Reluctantly, George shook it. Yet the amused twinkle in Llewellyn's eyes brought the blood racing back to George's cheeks. Was he taking the piss? Or was he just a happy, ever-grinning idiot? Hard to tell. In either case, he didn't like it. He didn't like it one bit. But what could he do? Too late to back out now. Shit, if only Davo were here.

"Okay," George said. "We've got a single window of opportunity. One chance to make national—perhaps international—headlines. We take it today or miss it. The head honchos from Clout Energy Drinks aren't going to visit the lab again. I know this on good authority."

"We're running out of time," Hannah said. "Take us through the plan."

George strode into the kitchen. They followed. On the table lay a printed Google map.

"This is Fraser University," he said, pointing at a clutch of buildings, "located in Melbourne's northeast. It's half an hour further out from La Trobe University. Know it?"

"Sure," Llewellyn said. "A mate of mine runs the vegetarian café at La Trobe."

"No, I meant Fraser University. You know it?"

Llewellyn shook his head.

"It's pretty small," Hannah said. "About fifteen thousand students and just the one campus. Compare that with La Trobe. They've got about thirty-five thousand all up."

"Yeah, cool. What are the main streams at Fraser?"

"What do you care?" George said. "You want to apply?"

"Curiosity, mate."

"Killed the cat."

Llewellyn smirked. "And satisfaction brought it back."

"They do science," Hannah said. "Biology, mostly. Genetics, animal health and disease, biochemistry, molecular biology, that kind of thing."

"Satisfied?" George said.

The bastard smirked again. George bristled. *Fuck that smarmy attitude.*

Hannah touched him lightly on the arm. "Tell us the plan."

He turned his attention to the map. Pointing, he said, "The grounds of Fraser University butt up against the Yarra Ranges. See that big green wedge opening up behind the ranges? That's the Alpine National Park. Beyond that is the Kosciuszko National Park. Combined, they make about seventeen-thousand-square kilometres, give or take. A perfect environment for the Tasmanian tiger."

Hannah said, "Plenty of rats, wallabies, and birds to eat."

"Sweet. Yeah, sounds good."

"I know it does. That's because it's my plan." From underneath the larger map, he brought out another. "Here's a close-up of Fraser. See this building on the eastern side of the main car park, shaped like the letter T? That's the Resurrection Lab. Our target."

Hannah murmured, "No animals should ever be kept in cages."

George pressed his thumbnail into the paper. "Pay attention. See this bit, the top line of the T-shape? The offices are at one end, labs at the other. And the long line of the T? That's where they keep the Tasmanian tigers."

"In cages," Hannah said.

Llewellyn curled his lip.

"This is how the shit's gonna go down," George said. "We bust into the Resurrection Lab. Once inside, I'm in charge. Is that clear? Hannah, you control the offices. Llewellyn, you take the labs. Once we've secured everybody in the building, taken their phones, maybe locked them inside one of the rooms, we go and free the tigers."

"How many people?" Llewellyn said.

"Huh?" George felt flustered. "I'm not sure. Maybe twenty."

Unexpectedly, Llewellyn crossed his arms and shook his head.

"What's the matter, Einstein?" George said. "Did I go too fast for you?"

"Nah, I'm just thinking..."

"Thinking what?" Hannah said.

"We ought to do this at night when there's a skeleton staff."

"Are you crazy?" George said. "Do it hush-hush? What for? The scientists might decide to keep the break-in quiet. Then what? We'll lose the publicity."

Llewellyn sucked at his teeth. "Guns and people, mate. Not a good mix."

"We're not shooting anybody," Hannah said. "It's just for show."

George slammed his palm on the table. "We want maximum exposure. If we bail up important people from Clout Energy Drinks at gunpoint, every single newspaper and TV channel is going to run with this story. Clout will make sure of that."

"This is about the tigers," Llewellyn said. "Not fame."

George's cheeks burned. *Shithead.*

Hannah said, "Listen, it makes sense to do things George's way. If we make headline news, we inspire other activists. It's a win-win." She patted the pocket of her denim jacket. "I've got the press release right here on my phone, ready to send as soon as we're done."

Victory. George saw acquiescence in the shithead's body language, in the way he dipped his head at Hannah. *But he ought to be deferring to me*, George thought, *not her. I'm the goddamned mastermind.*

"All right, Hannah," he said. "Did you nick your gran's rifle?"

She went to the lounge and retrieved her duffel bag. Unzipping it, she brought out the .22. Apparently, her grandmother lived on a wheat farm and hated cockatoos. And apparently, the grandmother was so old and had so many firearms that she wouldn't miss just one. But the rifle looked worn and warped.

"Does it still work?" George said.

"Oh, sure. The sight's a little skewed, but that doesn't matter. I mean, it's all about intimidation. We're not pulling any triggers."

Turning to Llewellyn, George sneered, "And how are *you* planning to intimidate?"

Llewellyn reached into the pocket of his vinyl jacket and brought out a .40 caliber Smith & Wesson semi-automatic pistol.

Holy Jesus.

Sweat broke out on George's forehead.

What a beauty. Matte black, ten-cartridge capacity, preferred firearm of the police and military. He had never seen the gun in real life before. His palm itched to hold it, but he would never lower himself to ask.

How did such a dipshit get his hands on an incredible firearm like that?

As if reading his mind, Llewellyn chuckled and said, "Don't ask."

For the first time since opening the front door, George stopped to consider. He didn't know the first thing about this prick. He could be a serial killer—or a copper—and George wouldn't have the slightest idea. Hannah was a different story. He'd known her for almost two years, had demonstrated by her side at plenty of events, admired her freckles and pale lashes, her youth and naivety. But Llewellyn? A wild card.

This skinny little bastard was a wild card.

***

Hannah drove and George rode shotgun, relegating Llewellyn to the back seat. The radio in the old, rusty hatchback didn't work, so George had no choice but to focus on every creak and squeak the car made as it rattled along Warburton Highway.

"I've never been out this way before," Llewellyn said. "It's real pretty."

This far east of Melbourne's CBD, Warburton Highway was a single carriageway, one lane in each direction, with dirt instead of concrete kerbs on the shoulders. The occasional weatherboard house peeked through the stands of eucalyptus, pine and wattle trees. Dead ahead was the bluish haze of the Yarra Ranges. A high cloud cover obscured the winter sky. At least it wasn't raining.

George checked his watch.

They were getting close.

His stomach churned with a sudden nervous jag. If only he could smoke. But Hannah wouldn't let anybody light up inside her car, not even George. The revolver pressed hot and sweaty into the small of his back. He should have taken it from his waistband before sitting down. Damned if he'd take it out now, with dickhead watching from the back seat.

Jail time.

If he got caught, George would face jail time over this assignment on account of the gun. From the beginning, he had prepared himself for the possibility. Now he felt scared. But how else would he become a counter-culture leader if not through martyrdom? Jail time would be a *good* thing. People would petition for his early release. Australia would soon realise that anyone who disagreed with George's philosophy stood on the wrong side of history. He took a deep, steadying breath.

The road sign ahead: FRASER UNIVERSITY NEXT LEFT 200 METRES.

Hannah took the turn-off. George bit at a knuckle, stopped when he remembered Llewellyn could see him.

Another road sign: WELCOME TO FRASER UNIVERSITY.

"Here we are," Hannah said, and gasped out a tremulous little giggle.

The driveway was a long, winding road lined with grass verges and trees. They passed the turn-off to a line of bus stops, the asphalt painted red. A few students milled around, walking singly or in groups, all wearing some kind of backpack.

Llewellyn released his seatbelt and sat forward, holding onto the front seats. "Do we know where to park?" he said.

"It's under control," George said. "Don't worry yourself, kid."

They rounded a bend and saw a parking lot coming up, jammed to the gills with cars.

Llewellyn said, "Are we gonna buy a ticket?"

"Of course," she said. "I can't afford any fine."

"Are you kidding me?" George said. "Hang on, bypass this parking area, we want the next one. Seriously, Hannah, we can't buy a ticket."

"Huh? Why not?"

"Because our only option is a Pay by Plate meter. Fuck that. To buy the ticket, you've got to enter the car rego. We may as well just call the cops on ourselves."

She frowned, crinkling her nose. "I don't want to get a fine."

"Look, there's not gonna be any inspectors," George said. "Students are poor, right?"

She lapsed into silence, still frowning. The road passed by various buildings, walking paths, natural planting areas, plenty of students on foot.

"Jeez, it's so clean," Llewellyn said. "I haven't seen a single piece of litter so far."

George sat bolt upright and flung out his arm, pointing. "There it is," he panted. "The Resurrection Lab. That building right over there."

"The one that looks like a concrete block?" Hannah said. "Or the other one?"

"Concrete block. With the flat roof and tinted windows."

Hannah slowed the car and turned into the side street. "Where do you want me to park?" she said. "Out front?"

"Yeah, but do a lap first. I want to see what's behind the animal pens."

The rear of the building had a high concrete barrier without any gates. Shit.

"All right," George said. "We can't get the tigers out the back way. We'll have to lead them through the lab and out the main door."

Llewellyn chuckled. "Hey, they're tigers, mate. We'll get bitten."

"Tigers in name only," George said. "They're about as dangerous as lambs."

"Okay, mate. You're the boss."

Damn straight.

Hannah brought the car around to the front of the building and braked. Her face looked white and pinched, eyes wide and startled. Shit, her nerves felt contagious.

"You okay?" George whispered, his throat suddenly dry.

"Yes," she said, and cut the engine. "Let's do this."

26

3

Bill De Vries may have been coming up to his fiftieth birthday, but he never tired of how people reacted when meeting him for the first time. His nicknames included Bear, Treetop, and Big Foot. Oh yes, he was a shock to the system, all right. Six-foot-six-and-a-quarter tall, over three-hundred pounds (his doctor wanted him to lose seventy, but naturally, a man Bill's size has a ferocious appetite), and a hand span wide enough to grasp a basketball. And this prim little old lady in the specs and lab coat had reacted just like everybody always did—by baulking, stepping back, mouth opening and closing in amazement.

Bill smiled, waited, and let her get used to the idea of him.

Meanwhile, his assistant, Simon, covered up his laughter with a pretend coughing fit. This scene never got old for Simon either, and he had worked for Bill some twenty years.

"Goodness gracious," the old lady said. "You're certainly a very tall man, aren't you?"

"That's what they tell me."

She glanced at the other woman standing next to her, the middle-aged Asian lady in a lab coat who had met Bill and Simon at the front door, and both women tittered. From nerves, probably. As the company axe-man, Bill was used to this reaction. His feet ached. He wanted to sit down. What was this room anyway, where they ate lunch? Didn't these eggheads have a proper boardroom somewhere?

Strike one.

Although, to be honest, the game was already fixed. His visit was nothing more than a formality. The crossing of a few T's, the dotting of I's.

He offered his hand. The old lady took it and startled. Oh yes, he loved this bit too: the shock on the face of anybody shaking with him for the first time. Apparently, it felt like a baseball mitt had swallowed your hand, whole, right up to the wrist. Bill had no way of knowing since he'd never met anyone bigger than himself to shake hands with.

"I'm so very pleased to meet you, Mr Pappas," the old lady said.

The Asian standing next to her made a small *ahem* noise. "Rosie—" she began.

"My name is Rosie Giuliani, professor of palaeontology, specialising in conservation biology and de-extinction. I'm head of the Resurrection Lab here at Fraser University."

"And I'm Bill De Vries, company accountant for Clout Energy Drinks."

"Oh." Pausing, withdrawing her hand, cheeks turning pink, the old lady turned to Simon—what a joke!—and said, "My apologies, Mr Pappas. I just assumed—"

"Rosie," the Asian interrupted again.

"He's not the managing director either," Bill said, brushing aside Simon's outstretched palm. "That's just Simon, my assistant."

In lieu of shaking, Simon chose to bow slightly from the waist, making himself look ridiculous. Was the little guy trying to show off his Friar Tuck hairstyle? Or did he assume the Asian woman was Japanese? Either way, it felt awkward.

"Let's sit down," Bill said, "and sort out this misunderstanding."

He took the chair at the head of the table.

God, his feet hurt.

The others sat around him. The old lady—Rosie—gazed at him expectantly, anxiety in her eyes. Nonetheless, she was the first to speak and her voice sounded firm.

"I was under the impression that Tony Pappas, managing director of the Australian office, would be visiting us today," she said. "That's what I was told."

Bill tutted. "Not a chance. The big boss over in the good old US of A decided to cut out the middle man. This issue is about funding. Who better to send than the man who controls the purse strings?" He touched his chest with his thumb a couple of times. "I run this show."

He leaned back and grinned.

Rosie and the Asian—was it Linda?—didn't smile back.

That bit about the "big boss" directive was an embellishment, naturally, but the upshot remained the same: to double-check that scratching the sponsorship was a good idea. Already he knew it to be true. Why was the lunchroom table empty? It should have platters of meats and cheeses, olives and artichokes, cut sandwiches. Where were the bottles of wine? Amateurs.

"So," he said, spreading out his hands. "Show me what you've got."

***

The dead thing in the jar made Bill feel sick.

About the size of a cat, the corpse, eyes closed, was folded in two as if crushed by careless hands, the jar filled with a yellow-tinted liquid. Bill swallowed. The back of his throat tasted like the bacon and eggs he'd eaten on the plane down from Sydney.

"This is Tommy," Rosie said, touching the jar lid reverently.

A couple of young blokes had put the jar on the lunchroom table and left. Bill wanted to leave too, but no, he would stick out this disgusting presentation for the sake of professionalism. Linda stood next to Rosie wearing a Mona Lisa smile that irritated him.

"The thylacine—Tasmanian tiger, sorry—went extinct about eighty years ago," Rosie said. "Most specimens were kept in formaldehyde, a chemical which degrades DNA. Intact DNA is more likely to be found from specimens pickled in alcohol."

"Okay," Bill said, waving his hand. "Let's move along."

Her face went pink but she didn't miss a beat. Tough old broad.

"Back in 1999," she said, "Professor Mike Archer and his team at the Australian Museum in Sydney attempted the first extraction of viable DNA from a thylacine foetus preserved in alcohol. The technique was somatic cell nuclear transplantation, the same technique used in our lab. Unfortunately, their DNA turned out to be unusable. Too degraded, too fragmented."

Simon was taking notes.

"What are you doing?" Bill snapped.

Suitably chastened, Simon sat back and lowered his pen.

"Please," Rosie said. "This is very important."

"Sure, sure," Bill said. "Gloss over the boring bits for me, all right?"

Rosie leaned on the table and fixed him with a piercing, unblinking gaze. Was she challenging his authority? It sure seemed like it. He almost felt sorry for her.

"Nine years ago, we got Tommy," she said, "also pickled in alcohol. He was part of a deceased estate in Devonport, Tasmania. Thankfully, the lawyer had some wits about him. Instead of throwing the specimen away, he contacted the science department at the University of Tasmania, who then contacted us, knowing we would be interested."

Bill rubbed at his eyes. "Skip the back story."

"*Fine*. We retrieved viable DNA from a tooth. Using in vitro fertilisation techniques, we took an ovum—an egg, I'm sorry— from a Tasmanian devil, a fellow marsupial."

"Let me stop you right there," Bill said. "Is this exciting? Because Clout is about excitement. Thrills. Edge-of-your-seat action. Formula One, air racing, sky diving—"

"We removed the Tasmanian devil nucleus from the egg," Rosie continued, raising her voice, talking right over the top of him, "and replaced it with a thylacine nucleus."

Such audacity! He glanced at Simon, who looked transfixed, open-mouthed.

"In nature," she was saying, "the ovum contains half the DNA, the sperm the other half. At the moment of conception, the fertilised egg gains a complete set. Our thylacine nucleus already had a complete set because it came from Tommy, so to kickstart the egg—to trick it into thinking it had been fertilised, as it were—we passed a weak electric current through it."

Bill sucked his teeth. "Yeah, I don't get it."

"Hang on," Simon said. "This is incredible. I've read about this kind of thing. Dolly the cloned sheep, wasn't it? They cloned Dolly in the same way."

"Exactly," Rosie said. "Except it's trickier in our case because we're dealing with a dead donor, not a live one, and we're using cross-species cloning techniques. Therefore, most of the time, the electric current did nothing and the egg died. But every now and then, the jolt of electricity brought the egg to life."

"Just like Frankenstein's monster," Simon said, his voice full of wonder.

"What, you mean Boris Karloff?" Bill said. "I still don't get it."

"Electricity brought the monster to life too," Simon uttered, breathless, eyes wide. "Christ on a bike."

"Hey," Bill said. "Keep your shirt on."

Rosie said, "The kickstarted eggs behaved like naturally fertilised eggs and divided. However, most of the eggs died before the blastocyst stage."

Bill sighed. "At the what stage?"

"Blastocyst. It's very early in the process. Before the egg develops into an embryo."

"Yeah, look, you keep throwing around these words—"

"A few of them made it. These we transplanted, one apiece, into the reproductive ducts of our Tasmanian devils." Rosie turned to Linda. "Would you like to take over?"

Linda offered a smile. "Marsupials don't reproduce like mammals, like humans."

Bill tuned out and rubbed at his eyes some more. He'd got up at the ungodly hour of 5 a.m. to fly to Melbourne and hear this nonsense. God, if only he could take off his shoes. He had fallen arches. A recent X-ray had revealed osteoarthritis in both feet. And yes, gout too, but he was hardly about to give up alcohol. All he needed was to take off his shoes and massage his feet. Keeping his gaze on the window, he avoided the pale, wrinkled body of the dead pup in the jar. Linda was yabbering on and on.

"You should listen to this," Simon said. "It's amazing."

"I'm listening, go ahead," Bill said, waving a dismissive hand.

Linda beamed. "As I was saying, after about forty days, the neonate emerges from the genital tract. It's hairless and blind, the size of a jelly bean. That's when we transfer it to the pouch of the red kangaroo. The pouch of the Tasmanian devil is too small, you see. After six months, the tiger is big enough to leave the pouch."

"Dear God," Simon breathed. "Have these techniques actually worked?"

"Hey," Bill said. "Calm down."

"Oh, my word, our techniques have worked," Rosie said. "Would you like to see?"

Simon stood up so fast, his chair clattered.

Rosie and Linda exchanged satisfied glances. Well, not for long, Bill thought. Once he drew his red pen through an expense, it ceased to exist.

***

The animal enclosure stank like piss and shit. Bill held his nose. Rosie offered a polite laugh. Clearly, she hated his guts, was crawling solely for the money, and that amused him.

"You get used to the smell," she said.

"Maybe *you* do," he said. "Not me."

From a room at the end of the corridor appeared a man with a mullet hairstyle and khaki uniform.

"I'd like you meet Glenn Hart," Rosie said, waving at the bloke to hurry on over.

"He takes care of the animals?" Simon said. "Oh, I've got so many *questions*."

Bill set his teeth. Why was Simon mouthing off? Bill shot him a warning glance. By this time, Mullet Man had jogged over.

"G'day," he said, taking Bill's hand (without any shock at his size?) and then Simon's, shaking vigorously. "I'm rapt you could come out here for a look. Now let me show you my charges, starting with our beaut little girls, the Tasmanian devils, that—"

"Glenn, let's cut straight to the thylacines," Rosie said. "These gentlemen are in a hurry."

"Oh," he said, faltering, grin fading. "Oh, sure. No worries. This way, if you please."

Glenn led. Christ, how tight were those damned shorts? Bill followed, leaving the others to trail behind. His feet hurt. As soon as he spotted the metal bars, he relaxed and smiled.

"Ah, you keep the animals in cages," he said. "My daughter will be very disappointed."

In a flash, Rosie was hovering at his elbow. "I'm sorry? What did you say?"

"My daughter hoped this would be more of a free-range set up. Eva is a bit of a greenie, unfortunately. Takes after her mother. Hasn't got the brains for numbers."

"Good God. You told your *daughter* about our program?"

He stopped walking to glare at Rosie. With two hot spots flaring red on her cheeks, she met his gaze and didn't back down. He put his hands on his hips. She still didn't back down.

"Yeah, I told Eva, and my wife too," he said, "just in passing. What's your problem?"

"The signed non-disclosure agreement between our lab and Clout."

He rolled his eyes. "Ah, relax. It was nothing. A casual discussion at the dinner table with family, that's all."

"Oh no," Simon peeped, white-faced. "That's still illegal."

Was Simon actually siding with the old broad? Humiliating Bill in public?

Rosie's face hardened like a hatchet. "I was assured," she said, enunciating every syllable like an English schoolmarm, "that all Clout employees tasked with assessing our sponsorship had signed legally-binding agreements forbidding discussion of the Thylacine De-Extinction Program with anyone, including family members."

Bill waved a hand. "Ah, get over yourself."

"This is a serious breach—"

"No one cares, honey! Science isn't sexy, all right? Let me tell you something. You're done. Okay? No bull. Pack your test tubes. It's over. You are *done*."

A loud buzzer went off. They all turned towards the entrance door as it opened. Linda appeared. Her mouth was pulled into a terrified rictus, her eyes wild. A stir of adrenaline moved through Bill's chest even before he saw the gun.

The barrel of a revolver pressed against Linda's throat. She shuffled into the room. The gunman, holding her around the waist with his free arm, shuffled in after her.

"What is this, some kind of prank?" Bill said.

A second man entered the enclosure and propped the door open with a chair. This second man was short and slight, and wore a balaclava. He had a semi-automatic pistol in his hand. Casually, he aimed it in their direction.

"Please," Rosie said, "whatever it is you want, let my colleague go. I'm Professor Giuliani, head of this lab. You'll have our cooperation. Just let her go. Please, I must insist."

"*You* insist?" said the gunman who held Linda. "You, member of the ruling elite, upholder of coercive authority, are delusional. You're not in charge any more. *I'm* in charge."

That voice. Bill knew that voice but couldn't place it.

As he scrutinised the gunman, who was disguised with a beanie and bandanna, the gunman shrank back as if to hide behind Linda. The bandanna couldn't hope to cover the entirety of that dark and full beard. Then it clicked.

"Well, well, well," Bill sneered. "If it isn't George King."

"Oh, hi, Mr De Vries," the gunman said, mumbling. "I didn't expect to see you here."

"You know this man?" Rosie gasped.

"Sure, he's one of Eva's deadbeat friends." He scowled at George. "What the hell kind of stunt are you pulling? Let go of that lady."

After a moment, George complied. Linda, tearful, ran into Rosie's arms and sobbed. Rosie looked mean and hard, ready to tear George a new one. Bill had to admire her guts. She ought to be in business, not wasting her time with extinct animals.

"Get out of here, George," he continued, "and take your little friend with you before I kick both your arses."

"Sorry, mate," the second gunman said. "No can do. We're here for the tigers."

A girl whose long, ginger hair flowed out from under a mauve balaclava jogged into the enclosure, duffel bag on one shoulder, slung rifle on the other. "Okay, everybody's locked in the storage room. I got all their phones right here," she said, shaking the bag.

She approached Bill, Simon, Rosie, Linda and Glenn, and opened the bag in front of them. "Phones, please."

Bill said, "Are there any more bozos, George? Or is it just you and these two idiots?"

"Oh, hey," the girl said. "We're sharing names now?"

"Shut up, Hannah."

"You shut up, meanie," she said. "Okay guys, hand over your phones. Llewellyn, please get these people to cooperate."

The second gunman, Llewellyn, ambled over. "Phones," he said, and pointed his gun.

As everyone obeyed, it occurred to Bill that he might be in a great deal of trouble. What was the old saying? *Loose lips sink ships.* Damn, his own loose lips may have sunk his career. He could feel his blood pressure rising, his heart hammering. He should never have mentioned the Tasmanian tigers to Eva. Shit. And when he recognised her friend, George King, he should have kept his mouth shut. Pappas would surely fire him over this debacle. Oh, *shit, shit, shit—*

"Where are the tigers kept?" Hannah said.

"At the far end of the enclosure," Rosie said. "Why? What do you want with them?"

"To free them, of course," Bill snapped. "Good Christ, woman, are you thick as a plank? Can't you see these cockheads are animal rights activists?"

George cleared his throat. "Actually, I'm an anarchist."

"You're a bloody loser and a cretin!" Bill yelled.

"Calm down, folks," Llewellyn said, chuckling. "Let's go for a stroll and see the tigers."

At gunpoint, they moved along the cages past a bunch of red kangaroos. Linda had recovered her composure, sniffling loudly. Rosie's face was closed, unreadable. She wouldn't meet his eye. Bill's forehead broke out in sweat as he imagined explaining himself to Pappas.

"Listen, Rosie," he said. "You and your team agree not to tell my boss about my… indiscretion… at the dinner table, and I'll let you keep your funding. I swear on it."

But she wasn't listening. "If you release our thylacines," she said, "they'll die. Please. They're not habituated to the wild. They don't know how to hunt, find water, take shelter."

"Stop fibbing," Hannah said. "Doing that kind of stuff is natural. It's in their blood."

"No, you're wrong. They're not like insects or fish. Higher animals need to be taught."

"Shush. You're a nasty vivisectionist."

Maybe Bill could buy Rosie's silence with a personal gift of money. He was about to suggest this when he happened to glance into a cage. The sight of the giant beast within staggered him and set his pulse racing even higher.

"Christ on a bike," Simon said, voice choked.

"Wow." Hannah approached the bars of one cage. "They're a lot bigger than I expected."

"Don't stand too close," Glenn said.

"It's okay. Animals read auras. They know I mean well. Hey, I think this one likes me."

Where was George, the self-proclaimed leader of this lame bunch? Bill looked around. There he was, the dumb-arse, standing way in back, shoulders slumped, gun hanging by his side. Just as Bill had long suspected: all piss and wind. Eva's taste in friends was terrible.

Llewellyn, who had crossed to the wall that ended the corridor, tapped the barrel of his pistol against a mounted console, and said, "Control panel?"

Glenn nodded. He was sweating too, maybe more than Bill.

Llewellyn waved his gun in a *come here* gesture. "Open their cages. We're walking the tigers right out the front door with us."

Rosie stepped forward. "No. These creatures aren't tame."

"Open the cages."

"Thylacines were savage hunters," she continued, voice rising. "They'd track prey for hours or days, run them down, run them ragged. Please. They eat live prey, not carrion."

"Yeah, but they don't eat *people*," Hannah said. "Tassie tigers are as gentle as lambs. Everybody knows that. Right, George? And they deserve to be free."

Simon said, "But these aren't natural creatures. Look at them. They're mutated monsters."

Linda began to softly weep again.

Llewellyn pointed his gun at arm's length. "Open the fucking cages right now."

"Sorry, Rosie," Glenn said. "It looks like we're rooted one way or the other."

"Will they attack?" she whispered.

"I don't know. I hope not. You and Linda try to stay still."

"Ugh, drama queens," Hannah said. "You can't scare us."

Glenn crossed to the panel and flicked a few switches.

A low rumbling, and the six cage doors slid back on metal tracks.

Bill held his breath.

Nothing happened.

The tigers, each one as big as a goddamned pony, stood motionless. *Completely* motionless, like taxidermy specimens. It didn't seem natural. Perspiration gathered in Bill's armpits and ran down his sides. Jesus, their eyes were so *black*. As black as tar. Could they see? Were they blind? Seconds ticked by. Shit. Why weren't the blasted tigers *moving*? And each one happened to be standing in the exact same posture. How? Bill's nut-sack shrivelled into a tab of goose flesh.

"Hey, sweetie," Hannah crooned, entering the nearest cage. "It's okay."

"Stay back," Rosie hissed. "Please, for God's sake..."

The girl pulled off her balaclava and tossed it aside. She looked young, fresh-faced. Approaching the tiger, she made soft kissing noises, and reached out her hands.

Sweat poured in rivulets from Glenn's hairline. This, more than anything else, made Bill want to run. If the animal handler was frightened, then by Christ, everybody ought to be.

"Aren't you lovely?" Hannah murmured as she touched the beast, fondling its ears like you would those of a beloved pet. "You're so beautiful. Oh, are you tired? George, Llewellyn, check it out, he's tired. See? Look, he's yawning."

Grandma, what big teeth you have.

The beast's jaws opened wide, wider, wider still, to an astonishing angle, an *impossible* angle. Surely, the joints must have dislocated by now. Bill's heart lurched and flopped. *Look out,* he tried to yell but couldn't find his breath, couldn't draw any oxygen.

With a crunch, the jaws slammed shut on Hannah's skull.

4

Rosie jumped, flinched, clutched for the gold cross around her neck before remembering that she had taken it off and thrown it away years ago, decades ago, the day her husband had died and the Almighty God had died in her too, right there alongside the hospital bed.

Hannah shrieked again.

The thylacine, number six—T6—back-pedalled within the cage on soft, padded feet, dragging the girl by her head. Classic predator behaviour. T6 would take the girl into the furthest corner to consume her in privacy. Rosie's fists clenched, spearing nails into her palms as she fought against a nauseating wave of faintness.

Glenn darted forward, bless him, as if to rush inside the cage. *No.* Big mistake. Like disturbing a dog at its bowl, any interruption would be met with teeth.

"Stop!" she commanded, and her shout rang against the concrete floor and walls.

He stopped, terror and confusion in his eyes.

"T6 will attack you," she continued. "Shut the cage doors."

"But, Rosie—"

"Shut the cage doors *now*. And *you* there, boy with the gun," she said, glaring at the white-faced, trembling Llewellyn, who had at some point taken off his balaclava, dropped it to the ground. "Hurry! Shoot the thylacine. Shoot to kill."

Glenn fumbled with the switches on the control panel. With a grating lurch, the cage doors began to rumble—slowly, ever so slowly—along their tracks. Llewellyn failed to react. Frozen, he stared, slack-jawed, into T6's cage.

Dear God, the sounds coming from the cage were ghastly.

Hannah was mewling, panting hard. The sound of teeth scraping against bone twanged and shivered Rosie's nerves like the shriek of fingernails down a blackboard.

"Shoot!" Rosie ordered. "For heaven's sake, boy, shoot!"

"It's not loaded," the boy muttered.

Momentarily, Rosie felt herself blanch, swoon.

Not loaded...?

She shouted at the fat, bearded man, "You there! What about your gun? Answer me."

He lifted the gun, stared at it as if he had never seen it before. Then he shook his head.

Sweet Mary and Joseph.

All this... *chaos*... for nothing.

The girl's death for nothing. And yes, the girl would die. Was already dying. The fracturing of her skull bones sounded, perversely, like the crackling snap of a sheaf of dried spaghetti getting wrung between two hands. A shudder passed through Rosie. The cage doors had almost closed. Thank God for small mercies. The girl may have lost her life, but at least everyone else would be safe once the thylacines were locked behind bars.

"Get a jab stick," she said to Glenn. "We might save her yet."

At the last second, as slinky as cats, simultaneously as if it were just the one lithe beast caught in repeating mirrors, the five thylacines stepped from their cages right before the doors banged shut behind them.

Rosie's breath choked off in her throat.

The creatures were close enough to touch with outstretched hands.

Motionless, T1 seemed to appraise her with his jet-black eyes. His brothers, similarly postured, stared at her too. Fear ran through Rosie in jets, like rivulets of iced water.

"Glenn...?" she whispered.

"Don't move," he said through clenched teeth.

The big Dutchman, Bill De Vries, began gasping. "Now what?"

"Will they bite?" Simon said.

"Of course they'll fucking bite, you idiot," Bill hissed. "The girl's getting bit, isn't she?"

Linda began weeping again.

Glenn held out his palms to the beasts in a calming gesture, murmuring to them in a low, gentle voice, "Shh, it's okay, fellas. Everything is okay. Shh, now."

The thylacines winked their wet nostrils, sniffing. Rosie's pulse knocked in her ears. *We're prey*, she thought. A group of prey animals, of a size that would give any predator pause, yet prey all the same. The thylacines would assess their risk of failure, of injury, and react accordingly.

The girl stopped whimpering.

"Hannah?" said a man's voice.

It was the fat, bearded man: George King. He had taken off his beanie and scarf. His eyes bulged, yellow and thread-veined. The revolver lay at arm's length against his thigh, jittering, his body trembling. He staggered forward as if preparing to fall down in a dead faint.

"If you have bullets," Rosie said, "load your gun and shoot the thylacines. Do it now."

George's eyes were as wide as peeled eggs. A dark stain across his jeans showed that he had wet his pants. He seemed not to have heard Rosie. The thylacines swivelled their heads to watch his approach. When George got next to Llewellyn, he stopped, swaying, fighting for breath, and gazed into T6's cage.

"Hannah?" he moaned, his voice thick with tears. "Hannah, are you okay?"

"Call the police," Rosie said. "You've both got phones, haven't you? Answer me."

But George and Llewellyn remained silent, dazed, stupefied.

"Answer me!" she snapped.

"They're in shock," Glenn said. "Tell me how you want to handle this."

At the far end of the corridor, the door which led to the rest of the building was propped open by a chair.

"We have to lock the enclosure," she said. "If they get loose in the building, the automatic doors will let them out onto campus grounds." Oh, the carnage… she couldn't bear the thought.

"Yeah, but how are we gonna lock down the enclosure from here?" Glenn said.

Good point. The enclosure door was some fifty metres away. It may as well be fifty kilometres. What to do? She had to *think*. All of her colleagues trapped inside the storeroom. Everyone's mobile in Hannah's bag, currently trapped—along with poor Hannah's corpse—inside T6's pen.

In the silence came the pop and snap of the girl's skull, the lap and slurp of a wet tongue. Rosie's stomach turned over. Linda put her face in her hands and wept hard.

"Listen carefully, all of you," Rosie said. "Behind us are offices. As a group, when I say go, back up. Stay together. They're less likely to attack if we stay together. Once inside the offices, we'll call for help on the landlines." She looked at Glenn. "We must close the enclosure door. You get the jab sticks."

He nodded.

"After I call the police, I'll help you sedate the animals."

"You're talking about tranquillisers?" Bill said. "How long till they work?"

"Five minutes, tops," Glenn said.

"Five *minutes*?" Bill rasped. "Fuck. We don't have five *seconds*."

He was right. The thylacines had advanced. Silently, with no growling or barking, their tails stiffened and held straight out.

"Go," Rosie whispered. "Start backing up."

Simon let out a sob. "You fucking *morons*," he shouted at George and Llewellyn in a sudden, howling rage. "I'm going to sue you. I'm going to sue you both so bad that your children's *children* will be penniless."

"I'm saving animals," Llewellyn said. "What are *you* doing? Eating them?"

The thylacines became short mouthed, their flews retracting.

"Quiet," Rosie said. "They're getting ready to bite. Grab a wallet, purse, anything you've got. Shove it into their mouths when they lunge. Keep backing up."

Simon's laugh sounded high-pitched, hysterical. "Oh, you stupid, self-righteous *pricks.*"

Llewellyn pointed at him with his gun, lips twisted in preparation to retort. A thunderous *bang* sounded, ringing concussively, painfully loud, against the concrete surrounds. Simon dropped. Everyone froze. The thylacines stopped and flattened their ears.

Simon was lying on his back. A wet, red patch flowered across his shirt.

It took a moment for Rosie to register what had happened.

"You shot him," she said, breathless and dazed.

"What? No, I didn't."

"Well, he's lying there dead," Bill bellowed. "How else do you explain it?"

Linda sobbed and wailed.

"But the magazine's empty," Llewellyn said, pulling the trigger, over and over. *Click, click, click, click.* "See? Empty."

"There must have been one in the chamber," Glenn said.

Llewellyn blinked. "Oh, shit…"

"Back up, everyone," Rosie said. "Hannah and Simon are dead. We can't help them."

In concert, the thylacines attacked.

Such wide jaws, big teeth, maws like that of great white sharks. Screams echoed throughout the enclosure. Rosie, blind with panic, turned and sprinted towards the nearest open door. The hem of her lab coat pulled and ripped. Her shoes skidded on the flat nap of carpet. She staggered to one knee. Linda fell and landed full-length on the floor beside her.

A thylacine—Rosie couldn't tell which one—closed in. She regained her footing and pushed the door shut. *Too late*. The thylacine leapt, mouth agape. But no, thank God, the latch caught in time. The beast hit the other side of the door with a heavy thud. Gasping, Rosie sagged to the carpet, reached out to Linda, and patted the sobbing woman's arm.

"It's okay, we're okay," she said, and looked about the room.

Oh, no.

Where was everyone else?

Outside were shouts, yelps, the ululations of thylacines. Clutching onto furniture, Rosie groped to her feet. She and Linda happened to be in Glenn's main office. A landline sat on the plywood desk. Lunging, Rosie snatched the handset and mashed at buttons.

The bland ringtone sounded in her ear.

"Campus security," said the bored male voice.

"This is Professor Rosie Giuliani. Armed terrorists breached the Resurrection Lab. Our lab animals have escaped. Everyone on campus is in danger. Call the police."

Silence.

"Hello?" Rosie shouted. "*Hello?*"

"Terrorists?" the male voice said. "Hang on, there's a bomb? Or what?"

"No, not a bomb." Rosie's teeth clenched so hard they might crack. "Listen to me. Our lab animals are loose. Send a message over the PA that everyone on campus is to remain inside. And call the bloody police. We need trackers. We need the dog squad."

45

"Lab animals? Wait a minute. What animals are you talking about?"

"Thylacines," she yelled. "Tasmanian tigers. For God's sake, call the police."

"Hey, is this some kind of joke?"

Rosie threw the handset at Linda and said, "Talk to security. Tell them. *Convince* them."

Wiping her nose, sniffling, Linda picked up the handset. "Hello?" she stammered.

Rosie went to the door. It was solid particle-board with no window. She opened the door a crack. Simon lay on the floor in a puddle of his own blood. Rosie swallowed a choke of tears, of terror. She had to keep a clear head. Opening the door wider, she peeked outside.

The enclosure's corridor was empty.

She stepped from the office, shut the door, and checked every room. Nobody. She ducked into the supply room. The two jab sticks were missing. Glenn must have taken them both, as instructed. She armed herself with a mop. Heart in her mouth, she hurried down the corridor. The Tasmanian devils kept shrieking their evil-sounding, demonic rasp.

Llewellyn's pistol lay on the ground. After taking a few steps beyond it, she changed her mind, went back and picked it up. She had never held a gun before. It felt lighter than she had anticipated. Pocketing it, she headed to the enclosure door, which was still propped open by a chair. A shiver ran through her. Oh, dear God...

Where were the thylacines now?

***

When the tigers attacked, George had found a speed in his legs that he'd never before thought possible. Hollering, he sprinted along the corridor. His buttocks and the backs of his thighs felt naked, hypersensitive, the flesh shrivelling in anticipation of sharp teeth. Llewellyn bolted past him, taking the lead. *Shit*. Wait, it was okay—Mr De Vries grunted and bellowed from the rear. The tigers would pull *him* down first.

George was almost at the enclosure's open doorway. A moment of euphoria. Goddamn, he was actually outrunning *a pack of tigers*. Gut or no gut, his reserves of physical power must be incredible. Two tigers dashed past him in pursuit of Llewellyn. No, not dashing—more like trotting at a leisurely pace. They yipped, tossed their heads, tongues lolling in doggy grins, excited by the tumult like a couple of puppies enjoying a romp.

Nevertheless, George couldn't stop screaming.

Once out the door, Llewellyn turned left. The two tigers followed him. Fuck that for a joke. George turned right, pinwheeling both arms to keep his balance as his boots skidded on the linoleum. Closed doors lined either side of the hall. No time to slow down and try the handle of each one. What if they were locked? What if the remaining three tigers ran at his heels? Dead ahead was a pair of swing doors, separated top to bottom by a thin, unbroken crack. *No locks.*

He burst through the doors, pulled up fast, and closed both doors behind him. Shaking, he braced himself against them. Any moment now, a tiger would try to push inside. Distant shouts and yells sounded. Llewellyn and Mr De Vries were heading towards the offices. Which meant that George must be... he opened his eyes... in one of the labs.

Equipment. So much equipment.

Three rows of desks ran lengthwise, one row against each wall, and the third down the middle of the room. Each desk had a chair and was topped with a hutch of shelving units. Computer monitors, scales, bottles, racks of test tubes, so many devices and tools he didn't recognise. Appliances that looked like faxes or old-fashioned teletext machines. Some big, clunky glass cabinets that contained what appeared to be giant pipettes hanging from revolving spice racks. *Nerdsville.*

Panting, he wiped the sweat from his brow and tucked the gun into the waistband of his jeans. He should have loaded the fucking thing at home when he'd had the chance.

From the other side of the double-doors: silence.

He turned and put an eye to the crack. No sign of any tigers. They hadn't followed him after all. Relief turned his knees to jelly. But he didn't feel safe. He needed to be behind a door with a lock on it. Better yet, he wanted out of this fucking place. Hannah always left her car keys in the ignition. Her mum had insured the hatchback for more than it was worth, and Hannah was forever hoping that someone would steal it.

George's heart cramped into a little ball. Hannah. Oh, Jesus... *Hannah.*

No time for tears. He had to find a way out. Surely, there would be an exit somewhere from this lab. He'd find it and run straight to the car. But his legs, shivering, wouldn't move.

Shit, this assignment had turned into a complete fucking *disaster.* And George was definitely going to jail. No ifs or buts. When Eva De Vries had told him about the Tasmanian tigers, she'd said the managing director of Clout Energy Drinks, a bloke called Tony Pappas, would be visiting the Resurrection Lab today. Pappas had never met George, wouldn't have been able to identify him. What the hell was Eva's *father* doing here?

Mr De Vries hated George.

Called him a slob.

Whenever George dropped by to see Eva, Mr De Vries made a point of asking him about his employment status. *Got a job yet, Georgie Boy?* What an arsehole. *Still hanging off the taxpayer's tit, Georgie Boy?* Aw, hell. If he'd known that Mr De Vries would be here, the assignment would not have gone ahead.

Another realisation occurred, one that made George groan: no one would ever praise him as a counter-culture leader. Not after this debacle. Not with Hannah and Mr De Vries's assistant dead. Tears rose. What a nightmare. What an utter, fucking nightmare.

Time to get out of here. He put his eye to the crack and checked the hall one last time. Still nothing. He willed his leg muscles to work. Tiptoeing, mindful of making any sound that might draw the attention of the tigers, he crept away from the swing doors and headed between two rows of desks. He glanced at the ceiling, hoping for a green glowing EXIT sign. No such luck. Shit, there *had* to be a way out of here. To hell with running the gauntlet of that long, long hall to the automatic doors at the far end. Fuck that.

A swishing noise. Startled, George halted and spun around.

One of the doors to the lab had opened.

It was Llewellyn, red-eyed, tears and snot running down his face, distraught.

"Hey, mate," he called, his voice catching on a sob. "Are you in here? I need to talk."

George hissed, "Shut the fucking door!"

Llewellyn shuffled into the lab. "Oh, this is so not cool. I'm a pacifist, mate. A *pacifist*."

Blood rushing hot to his face, George hurried to close the door. Two tigers were strolling the hall towards him. The sight almost stopped his heart. Forgetting the door, turning on his heel, he ran on rubber legs until he lost his footing a few seconds later. He crawled over the floor, dragged out a chair, and tried to huddle beneath a desk. His backside hit the wall. He pulled the chair in after him.

Llewellyn got down on hands and knees to peer at him, perplexed and tortured.

"Mate, I'm broken up," he said, lips quivering. "I don't even kill huntsmen spiders. You know what I mean? I catch them in my hands and take them outside. You feel me, mate?"

"Shut up."

"I don't use fly spray either."

"Tigers!"

"And now I've killed a man. How can I get my head around it?"

"Shut the fuck up!"

Llewellyn gazed at him with questioning eyes, tears streaming one after the other.

Behind Llewellyn, the tiger appeared in mid-air as it bounded, like a kangaroo, some six feet up and over the hutch of shelving. George shrieked. The tiger landed, all four paws, on Llewellyn's back, knocking him flat to the ground and punching the air from his lungs in a loud retch. The jaws closed around the nape of his neck. Llewellyn's face showed confusion and pain, but no fear. As if the poor bastard didn't know what had hit him.

Muscles bunched in the animal's chops as it bit down. Blood spurted in multiple jets. *Like a lawn sprinkler*, George thought in a horrified daze. A sprinkler turned on full bore.

The tiger shook at Llewellyn's neck. Coming to life, Llewellyn thrashed his arms and legs, smearing blood in ever-widening circles on the linoleum, forming a grisly Spirograph pattern, around and around and around. His mouth opened and closed, trying to scream. Only blood came out in a long, continuous vomit.

George threw up coffee, curdled hash browns, pancakes, and imitation maple syrup.

Looming, the tiger stood on its hind legs. Llewellyn dangled from its mouth, limbs flailing. The only sound was the steady pattering of blood against the linoleum. George was trapped under here, trapped against the wall. He had to get out. Had to get out *now* before the tiger lost interest in Llewellyn.

With a strangled cry, George shoved out the chair and scrambled to his feet. He ran towards a door that stood ajar. The sign read TOILET. He caught a last glimpse as he slammed the door: the tiger, enormous, standing upright; the limp and bloodied rag of Llewellyn, still held by the neck, head hanging at an impossibly crooked angle.

Jesus fucking *Christ*.

Heaving, sobbing, George leaned his forehead against the door and shook from head to toe. He opened his eyes. White tiles. White sinks next to him. Soap dispensers. A mirror. The bathroom stank to high heaven of shit. It took him a few seconds to realise the smell was coming from *him*. At some point during the tiger's attack on Llewellyn, George had crapped himself. Well, at least he could clean up in here. And then wait for the cavalry to arrive. In fact, he'd call the police himself. He patted his pockets for his mobile.

And heard it.

Soft, regular breaths. Coming from behind him.

The rush of adrenaline jerked his body and banged his nose against the door. Gasping, he peeked over his shoulder.

The other tiger.

Two had entered the lab. How could he have forgotten the other one?

It stood on its back legs and towered over him. The golden fur was so short that every formidable muscle in the tiger's chest, shoulders, and front legs showed in sharp relief. A bulge of veins crisscrossed its torso. George's last coherent thought was of Davo, his bodybuilder friend. If only Davo had come on this assignment instead of Llewellyn, none of this would be happening. The tiger fixed George with its huge, wet and black eyes.

Flews pulled back. Jaws opened. Strings of drool stretched between the teeth.

The tip of the long, red tongue waggled. Slowly, ever so slowly, the tiger tipped its massive head to one side. George clutched at the door handle. But the door opened inwards. The tiger loomed too close. The jaws advanced. George closed his eyes and screamed.

The pressure on his throat felt, at first, like a firm headlock. Firm enough to cut off his scream. The pulse thudded in his temples as the grip intensified. Teeth punctured his flesh. A hot flow of blood soaked his t-shirt. The final thought that registered in George's terrified mind was that his bowels had once again let go.

5

Bill ran into the lunchroom and slammed the door.

Safe.

The bastards had bitten him on the arse and legs. Gasping, he awkwardly reached around to pat at the back of his trousers. The fabric was torn. His hand came away bloody.

Oh, there'd be hell to pay for this, he thought, grinding his teeth. Simon was right. Lawsuits, left, right and centre. He'd persuade Tony Pappas to buy this shithole of a university just to sack everyone in it and burn the place to the ground.

Simon...

Lightheaded, Bill groped for a chair and sat. The bite wounds throbbed. He ran his bloodied palm down his jacket, over and over, but it still came away sticky. The kitchen sink was just a couple of metres away but he doubted his legs had the strength to carry him there.

Simon.

Dead.

It didn't seem feasible. Now what? After twenty years of service, Simon knew what to do without being told. Even anticipated Bill's requests. Who could replace him? Then again, Bill might not need an assistant. There was a fair chance Pappas would sack him for breaching the non-disclosure agreement, for tipping off those dickheaded activists.

Bill glanced up and startled.

That jar with the tiger pup was still on the table.

What a disgusting artefact. He shifted in his chair so as not to look at it. A familiar harsh, burning pain started up behind his breastbone. He rubbed at his chest with his knuckles. The old angina was acting up again. But Simon carried his pills. Fuck. *Fuck.*

The jar caught his eye.

Despite himself, Bill glanced at the wrinkled, mummified corpse suspended in the yellow liquid. He and his older brother had wagged school one day and found a sackful of drowned kittens down by the river. God, Bill hadn't thought about that in *years*. But this tiger pup had the same kind of crumpled, wet, and forlorn look. Bill pinched at the bridge of his nose, reached for his phone, then remembered that the stupid girl had taken it at gunpoint.

Oh God, the crunch of her skull bones breaking…

Panting, he gazed around the lunchroom, hoping for a landline. No such luck. What the hell was going on out there? Was anybody contacting the authorities? The pup's front paws were held together as if in prayer. From its mouth peeked the very tip of a blanched tongue. *Hey, catch*, Levi had said, jeering, throwing a kitten at him. Bill pulled at his tie, undid the top shirt button.

Damn, it was stifling in here.

Every window was sealed with silicone. A grey vent in the wall hummed and rattled. Nothing worse than sealed windows. A reverse-cycle air conditioning system just didn't cut it. Bill always drove with the car windows cracked a few centimetres, even in the rain. On planes, he had to take a mild sedative, practise his calming self-talk, ignore the windows. Simon always opted for the window seat without being told.

Simon…

The pup's tail had a sharp kink in it, as if broken. Perhaps the injury had occurred while the pup was alive. More likely, whoever had crammed the dead thing inside the jar had been careless, used too much force. *Snap.* The crunch of the girl's skull.

"For fuck's sake!" he bellowed. "Is somebody doing something about this situation?"

No answer.

He was stuck in this room and couldn't get out. It was too warm in here. There wasn't enough air. He couldn't breathe. Maybe he could take a chair and throw it through a window. *Hey, catch.* Bill rubbed at his chest, puffing, sweating, crying.

***

One of the swing doors to the laboratory was open.

Glenn advanced. He wielded both jab sticks. In the vet room, he had drawn a deliberate overdose into each syringe: ten ccs of combined ketamine and diazepam. Additional vials—all of them, in fact—were in his top pocket. He wore cut-resistant gloves. Not much good against needle-stick injuries or teeth but better than nothing. On his wrist, a roll of duct tape, worn like a bracelet. The open laboratory door was five metres away.

Now four, three...

Adrenaline prickled throughout Glenn's body.

Careful, *careful.*

The tigers were as shifty as shithouse rats. Just because he couldn't hear anything didn't mean they weren't lying in wait. He checked over his shoulder again. The hall was still empty. Glenn hesitated at the open door. Take it easy. Don't blunder into an ambush. Relax.

He knew these animals, he *knew* them.

Relax.

Softly, flat-footed, stealthy, he moved through the doorway into the lab.

He saw the tiger straight away. With its back to him, it stood on hind legs. From its jaws dangled the skinny bloke, Llewellyn, motionless and soaked in blood. Dead. The tiger batted at the corpse with its front paws, as if playing. Glenn held his breath. Took a step, then another. Reflexively tightened his grip on the jab stick in his right fist.

Closer, get *closer*.

Standard, a jab stick was one metre long. Screw-in extension poles could have lengthened each stick to two metres. In the vet room, however, Glenn had decided against using the poles. Two metres? Forget it. Awkward to carry and deploy. But the tiger was a *giant*. Glenn regretted his decision now. Outside of a cage, one metre was too bloody short.

Okay, close enough to see the ear tag. Red. Tassie tiger number five, T5, the one he'd nicknamed Diesel. A few more paces. Just a few more. Relax. Blood covered the linoleum. This reassured him. With so much spilled blood, the tiger wouldn't smell him.

Glenn stepped into the gory puddle.

Don't slip.

Muscles rippled in the tiger's back. Llewellyn's corpse swung between the batting paws.

Glenn thrust out his right arm, hard, fast, like a javelin thrower going for the Olympic ninety-metre record, and stabbed the hypodermic needle into the meat of the tiger's buttock. The spring-loaded plunger activated. Ten ccs of tranquilliser injected in under a second.

Diesel reacted as if zapped by an electric shock.

With a frantic hop, its jaws closed hard enough to sever Llewellyn's neck. The head and body dropped to the floor in separate pieces. *Fucking hell.* Glenn ducked behind a row of desks. After dashing in a chaotic and tight circle, Diesel staggered and sat down hard. Huffing, snorting, mouth hanging open, its front legs slid forward. Its eyes blinked lazily, once, twice. A moment later, the tiger's head began to tilt.

You little ripper. Glenn's heart pounded in excitement.

After one final grunt, Diesel crashed onto its side, out for the count.

The urge to rush in was almost too strong to resist. Wait, Glenn thought. *Wait*. It could take a couple of minutes for the dope to take full effect. To pass the time, after checking his surroundings, Glenn decided to reload the jab stick. He pulled back and snapped shut the cocking lever to reset the spring, rotated the safety cuff to expose the syringe's plunger, and grabbed a vial. He stabbed the needle into the vial and drew another ten ccs, checking behind him all the while, keeping an eye on Diesel. Then he pocketed the vial and turned the safety cuff on the jab stick back to "fire".

The tiger snored.

Propping both primed sticks against a desk, Glenn took the roll of duct tape and muzzled Diesel. Next, he bound together its front and back legs. Diesel's breathing sounded ragged. Could ten ccs be a fatal dose? Glenn didn't know. The most he had ever given these animals was three ccs.

Picking up the jab sticks, he crept through the laboratory.

Man, he hadn't felt this alive in a long time. Not since he had worked for the open-range zoo. The male hippos had fought all the time. The two herds of impalas couldn't get along. Danger had been as commonplace as break-time coffee. He missed the excitement, he realised now. Looking after animals in cages wasn't the same.

Then he saw the blood.

Oozing from under the dunny door.

Whose blood? He didn't know. *Please don't be anyone on staff*. As soon as the thought struck him, Glenn felt ashamed. The knobs and greenies deserved to live too.

At the dunny door, he checked all around him.

Situational awareness was key.

During his years at the open-range zoo, he'd seen plenty of numpties get hurt by ignoring the surroundings. But not Glenn. He'd grown up on his aunt's crocodile farm. Those crafty reptiles kept you on your toes, all right. One minute as still as statues, the next snapping, trying to take your bloody arm off. Glenn turned the handle and pushed. The door resisted.

Through the crack, he could see a body on the floor, covered in blood: the fat greenie.

Yip, yip, yip.

Uh oh. Look sharp. Tiger. Glenn checked behind him. Coast clear. By keeping the door between them, he would be safe while jabbing the bugger and waiting for it to zonk out.

But the tiger's muzzle rammed through the gap.

The door forced open. The tiger shouldered through the doorway. Its mouth was agape, eyes as black as pitch. Glenn tripped, fell backwards, feet scrabbling.

I'm going to die.

The tiger lunged.

Glenn rammed both needles into it. One found a leg, the other the chest. The springs that depressed the plungers went off. As the tiger writhed and struggled, Glenn gripped the sticks, keeping them upright with every ounce of strength. These sticks, braced against the floor, were the only things keeping the tiger at bay, a scant metre distant above him. The tiger craned its neck. Teeth closed in. Drool slopped on Glenn's chin.

Oh God.

Those teeth.

Eyelids flickering, the tiger collapsed. Glenn's strength ran out. Both jab sticks fell sideways and he let them go. To resist might break his arms.

The weight of the tiger landed across him, heavy as a tipped brick wall. Shit, he couldn't move. Was the tiger still conscious, still able to bite? The next few seconds felt agonising, excruciating. Then the tiger began to snore. Glenn exhaled.

Fuck me dead, he thought, trembling. So much for his vaunted "situational awareness." His years working at the Resurrection Lab must have blunted his reflexes. He had to lift his game. Next time, he might not be so lucky.

The snoring tiger weighed a ton.

With some effort, he dragged himself free. It was T3, according to the yellow ear tag. The tiger he called Sparky. Glenn grabbed the roll of duct tape. His fingers trembled.

***

Apparently, Rosie's entire staff was behind this door. She drew back the bolt on the storeroom and peeked inside.

"Is everyone okay?"

"Oh, thank Christ," Indigo said. "The gunmen have left?"

"Let's get out of here," Michael said, pulling on the handle.

"Stop!" Rosie hissed. "They released the thylacines. Five of them are loose in the building. At least, I *hope* they're still in the building."

Indigo gasped, bringing a hand to her mouth.

"Fuck," Michael said.

"All of you, stay put," Rosie said. "Linda is on the phone to campus security."

She started to turn away.

"Wait a second, aren't you coming in with us?" Michael said.

"No. I have to deactivate the automatic doors and stop the thylacines from escaping."

Michael's eyes widened. Rosie shut the door to the storeroom.

The long hall was empty in both directions. Quiet. God, she felt naked. Vulnerable. Just a mop and an empty gun with which to defend herself. She needed a shield of some kind.

Her crepe-soled flats didn't make a sound on the linoleum. She ducked into an office and grabbed a high-backed swivel chair on casters. Resting the mop on it, she pushed the chair out from the behind the desk, keeping the seat facing her. If a thylacine charged, she could use the chair to keep it at bay. If *two* thylacines charged, however…

She paused in the doorway to scan the hall. Her body shook. All she had to do was shut herself inside this office and she would be safe. Besides, the thylacines had probably exited the building already. Why take the risk? The instinct to stay and hide was almost too great.

Clenching her jaw to stop the chattering of her teeth, she rolled the chair out of the office. Fear stopped her from going any further. The automatic doors were so very, very far away. About twelve metres. The function panel near the jamb included a three-position switch marked AUTO/CLOSED/OPEN. The switch was currently in AUTO mode, which meant the doors operated via motion sensors. She had to flick the switch to CLOSED to shut both doors and keep them shut.

Checking behind her, she began to roll the chair along the hall.

The caster wheels made a smooth, trundling noise over the linoleum. Thylacines had excellent hearing. They would come to investigate. Would she detect their stealthy approach over the sound of her hammering pulse? There were so many open doors off this hall. A thylacine could be hiding in any one of these rooms, getting ready to pounce.

Her breath came and went in ragged gasps.

She should have euthanised this bloody litter a long time ago. As soon as the *oddness* of the animals had become apparent, she should have put them down at once. She managed a wry, bitter smile. Oh, how easy to say such a thing now, in retrospect. Hindsight is twenty-twenty. But she had wanted to study their abnormalities, figure out the causes so that the *next* litter would have a greater chance of turning out successfully, and she couldn't do that if—

A skittering sound from behind punched Rosie's heart into her throat.

With a cry, she spun around, gripping the chair's arms so hard that her knuckles cracked.

Nothing. The hall was empty.

But Rosie knew better. That sound had been strong, blunt thylacine claws tapping against linoleum. The animal had ducked into one of the rooms. Which one? So many open doors...

The psalm came unbidden: *Cast your cares on the Lord and he will sustain you; he will never let the righteous fall.* Old habits die hard. But, as a lapsed Catholic, she probably wasn't "righteous" enough in any case.

Backing up, Rosie darted her gaze from one doorway to another. She pulled the chair after her with one hand. In the other, she took up the mop. She glanced over her shoulder. The automatic doors were perhaps eight metres away and closing. Keep going. Almost there.

Yip, yip, yip.

Rosie jumped. That call had come from *behind* her, near the exit. She turned.

Nothing. The hall was empty in that direction too.

But it meant that a *second* thylacine was between her and the automatic doors. In one of the offices she had yet to pass.

Oh God. Oh, dear God.

Her limbs trembled. Which way should she face the chair? She couldn't decide. The answer depended on knowing which thylacine would attack first. And how could she know that, for Pete's sake? She felt hot, sweaty, dizzy...

No.

She must disarm the automatic doors and keep these two thylacines—perhaps more or even all *five* of them—inside this building. It was lunchtime. Outside, the campus would be teeming with lecturers, tutors, admin staff, and students descending on the food court plaza.

Lowering her head, she pushed the chair towards the automatic doors, running now, the casters rumbling, her shoes squeaking with every step, breath heaving in and out.

Yip, yip, yip.

Pulling up and turning in a sloppy half-circle, almost losing her footing and her control over the chair, she raised the mop handle. The tip of a tail disappeared inside a nearby office. Her blood chilled. *They were stalking her.* Thylacines were ambush as well as pursuit predators. The shape of their distal humerus at the elbow made that clear. These two—or three?—were playing like cats with a trapped mouse.

She rotated the chair once more and pushed it, as fast as she could go, towards the automatic doors. The control switch on the jamb was the only thing that mattered, the only thing she could see. It shone and shimmered through her tears. She covered the last few metres bumping and sliding against the wall so as not to activate the motion sensor, letting go of the mop to extend her shaking hand. The mop clattered to the floor. Her fingers touched the control switch.

Click.

The switch moved to CLOSED.

Thank God. She had *done* it. Relief took the strength from her legs. She fell to one knee. The deep, coughing bark of the thylacines lifted her head.

There were three of them.

They stood, side by side, in the doorway of Rosie's own office. The coincidence seemed deliberate, cruel and ironic. She stared into the black eyes of T1, with its black ear tag and extra-wide swipe of white fur on both cheeks, and she trembled. The mop was too far to reach. And what good would it do anyway? Perhaps Rosie could huddle into the corner here, pull the chair up against her with all her might… Yet a thylacine would only have to spring over the back of the chair to foil such a ludicrous plan.

No.

She was doomed.

A strange calm descended upon her. If there was a heaven—and she didn't know what she believed any more, since she dithered between atheism and agnosticism—she would be reunited with her husband. Rosie let go of the chair and sat on the floor.

There was nothing left to do now but wait for her creations to destroy her.

The thylacines dipped their heads, lengthened their necks, pulled back their flews to show gleaming, glistening sets of pointed teeth. All three began to hiss through closed jaws. Rosie clasped her hands and wept. It wouldn't hurt for long. Thylacines were efficient killers. The pain might last a minute or two and then her suffering would be over.

A door banged open with great force, startling her. The thylacines flattened their ears.

Good God, it was Bill De Vries, running out of the lunchroom, his face a mottled purple.

He was running down the hall towards her.

Towards the automatic doors.

The thylacines stopped hissing to stare at his clumsy approach. He ran at them as if he couldn't see them, his petrified gaze fixed straight ahead. Tie askew, his suit jacket flapping open, his enormous belly jouncing and rolling under his shirt, his heavy tread shuddering the floor. Blindly, he held both arms out in front of him.

"Stop!" Rosie shouted. "I've locked the doors!"

In reply, he screamed. A raw, terrified, animalistic bellow that set the thylacines howling.

Rosie clambered to her feet. "Stop! You can't get out this way!"

Bill De Vries ran full-tilt at the automatic doors and smashed through them in a mighty explosion of glass. Rosie shielded her face. When she looked up a moment later, De Vries was lying prone at the concrete entrance, surrounded by a snowfall of broken glass.

The exit was now wide open.

"Mr De Vries," she called. "How badly are you hurt?"

Stirred by the commotion, the thylacines dashed and leapt about the hall in great agitation, ululating and barking. And then T1 stopped to regard the exit, calm and thoughtful.

Rosie gasped. Oh no, no, *no…*

Outside was a roadway, a grassy strip containing a rockery with low-lying shrubs, other buildings. A cloudy sky, birds, a light breeze. And people. Lots and lots of people.

The two brothers fell quiet and watched T1, as if waiting for his cue.

They won't leave, Rosie decided. The world is a mystery to them. They've only known the enclosure. Fear will make them stay. She waited for them to pace, to start whimpering.

T1 lifted his muzzle and inhaled, long and loud. Rosie held her breath. With a lick of his chops, T1 trotted towards the open doorway. His two brothers followed.

"No!" Rosie cried.

They ignored her. The brothers picked their way carefully over the broken glass, sniffed without much interest at De Vries, and hesitated at the exit, looking around.

Come back, Rosie prayed. Oh, *please* come back.

They left the building.

Shit!

Scrambling on hands and knees, she crawled out from the wall to gape at the grounds of Fraser University. Already, the thylacines were nowhere to be seen. Damn. She grabbed De Vries's ankle and shook it.

"Can you get up?" she yelled.

"Nah, I reckon he's dead."

It was Glenn, wielding two jab sticks, panting as if he'd been running. There was blood on his uniform. His own? Rosie couldn't tell. He didn't appear injured. She clutched at his leg for a moment—desperately, in pitiful relief—and felt like weeping again.

"Three thylacines have escaped," she said. "And I'd only just locked the door…"

Glenn squatted next to De Vries and pressed two fingers against the man's throat. Then he shook his head.

"Nah," he said. "Cactus. The unlucky bastard probably had a heart attack."

"Can we do CPR?" The success rate was poor, yes, but surely, they had to do *something*.

"There's no way we can turn him over," Glenn said.

"We have to try."

"How? Crikey, just *look* at him. We'd need a forklift."

Oh, it was true. She gazed at poor Bill De Vries, at his bulk, at the massive and unshirted abdomen that spilled out on either side of him like a giant, pink cushion. *Lord, those who die still live in Your presence; their lives change but do not end.* She shook her head to clear it.

Glenn paused, chewed on his lip. "The other two greenies are dead as well."

She startled. "Oh, dear God."

"I've knocked out T5 and T3, got 'em hogtied in the main lab. So, what do we do now?"

What indeed? Her head was spinning. She could hardly think.

The sound of a bell indicated that an announcement was coming over the PA system.

"Attention staff and students," said the disembodied voice of the university's secretary. "Dangerous dogs are on the premises. Remain inside until further notice. I repeat, there are dangerous dogs on the grounds. Police are on their way. Stay inside."

"Well, that's a start," Glenn said, and offered Rosie his hand.

6

Pursing her lips, Senior Constable Janine O'Connell drummed her fingers against the steering wheel and tried to keep her impatience in check. One of the sergeants, Harvey Nussbaum, was on the phone. Harvey the panic merchant. He often rang her during her drive home, fretting about some trivial little thing or another. Weak, whiny people like Harvey pushed Janine's buttons, made her give short and irritated replies. She hated behaving this way but couldn't help herself.

"Tigers?" Janine said. "Bullshit. There are no tigers in Australia outside of zoos."

"Wait, not the big orange kind. Not tigers from Africa."

"Asia," she corrected.

"Yeah, whatever. Look, by all accounts, these escaped animals are *Tasmanian* tigers."

Janine rolled her eyes. A smattering of rain fell, in a hard and vicious handful, from the darkening sky. She flicked on the windscreen wipers and swept the droplets away.

"Someone's pulling your leg," she said. "Dingoes and Europeans killed off the Tasmanian tigers early last century. You mean brindle-coloured dogs. Pit bulls and boxers have stripes similar to a Tasmanian tiger. Contact the local pound."

"There's been, like, fifty calls to triple-oh already. More coming in every minute."

"Harvey, I'm almost home. I'm tired."

"You live right near Fraser University, don't you? People are freaking out."

"Harvey, students are always freaking out. It's literally their *raison d'être*."

"Look, would I ring you if it wasn't urgent?"

Yes, she thought, *and you do it all the time.*

She checked the rear-view mirror. Zeus, behind a grill in the station wagon's cargo area, stared out the window. The German Shepherd loved to watch trees whiz by on the Warburton Highway. As a puppy, Zeus had barked at trees whenever he had travelled in the car. Discipline and consistent training had encouraged stoicism. Now, his enthusiasm for trees showed only in the prick of his ears.

"Fair go," she said. "Zeus and I tracked a break-and-enter on overtime all morning."

"And found the mongrel, too."

"Naturally," Janine said, and smiled.

Over several hours, Zeus had tracked the kid, on foot, to a Hungry Jacks. The kid had been tucking into a burger when Janine had collared him, the backpack of stolen goods on the table—mobiles, jewellery, digital cameras, gift cards for various stores—a haul worth about twenty thousand dollars. The kid had walked a circuitous route, some fifteen kilometres, from crime scene to burger joint, for reasons unknown. Perhaps meeting up with drug dealers or fences along the way. That was for coppers in the Property Squad to figure out. Zeus had done his job and had received a treat of beef jerky. And now, Janine deserved a gin and tonic—or two—the bottles waiting for her on the kitchen sideboard.

"Janine, I'm short on general purpose dogs."

"Then reassign the day shift."

"I'm trying. Most are an hour away, minimum."

She sighed. Out of all the German Shepherds in the squad, only ten were general purpose trackers like Zeus. The others were specific to narcotics or explosives. Overtime may be nothing unusual, but she had to draw the line somewhere.

"My shift was supposed to finish at seven this morning." She glanced at the dashboard clock. "It's nearly half-past twelve."

"Yeah, but four people are confirmed dead so far."

Janine's eyebrows raised in horror and shock. "What? Say again. Four *dead*?"

"Yeah. I probably should have led with that intel, come to think of it."

"And the pit bulls killed them?"

"Details are pretty sketchy," he said. "We got the first call about ten minutes ago from a security guard, but it looks like a mob of escaped Tasmanian tigers are to blame. Uniformed coppers are converging on-site, plus ambos and what-not, but it's fucking turmoil, apparently. The campus is huge, people are panicking, getting chased, getting bitten. The tigers are hard to find. I need you to find them. Okay? Find them. Your contact is a Professor Rosie Giuliani. She's waiting for you out front of a building near the second car park. The building's called... hang on a sec, let me find the note... yeah, the Resurrection Lab."

The *Resurrection* Lab?

Janine felt a momentary prickle of unease.

A road sign came and went: FRASER UNIVERSITY NEXT LEFT 200 METRES. In the rear-view mirror, Zeus seemed bright, fresh and alert, despite the day's labours.

"On my way," she said. "ETA three minutes."

"Keep me posted. I'll do what I can to get you K9 reinforcements ASAP."

The call disconnected. The radio came back through the speakers. Janine switched it off.

"Zeus?" she said, and he looked around, tongue lolling. "We're not going home just yet."

Janine took the turn-off. After a minute, another sign: WELCOME TO FRASER UNIVERSITY. She drove along a meandering, single-lane entry road. On the other side of a median strip was the exit road, packed with a conga-line of cars, bumper to bumper, speeding and weaving. Janine cracked the window. Could she hear *screaming*?

Adrenaline fired, blasting away her fatigue.

"Heads up, Zeus," she said, tightening her grip on the steering wheel. *"Schwierigkeiten."*

She always gave Zeus his commands in German. It avoided confusion, particularly in chaotic situations involving many people talking at once. *Schwierigkeiten* meant "trouble."

The dog sat up straight, closing his chops and gazing intently out the windows. Janine wore her dark blue police uniform as she always did at the end of a shift, but was unarmed. Too bad Victorian police didn't have personal issue firearms. The first ten minutes of every shift involved signing out for a gun and other equipment such as taser, radio, collapsible baton and handcuffs, while the last ten minutes were spent signing the stuff back in again. If the dogs—tigers?—were dangerous, Janine had diddly squat with which to defend Zeus and herself.

The road wound back and forth on itself, hair-pinning through grassy median strips lined with eucalypts and acacias. She approached a car park on her left. People sprinted through it, scattering towards vehicles. Even from this distance, it was clear they were scared shitless.

Tension clenched Janine's body. She was built lean and stringy, a long-time fan of running, a shunner of junk foods and alcohol. Nearing her fortieth birthday, she looked no older than thirty. Physically, she was up for this challenge. Dogs, tigers, whatever, it didn't matter. She would protect and serve. Gun or no gun.

From the cargo area, Zeus began to whine in anticipation.

Janine passed the first car park, slowed to read the sign boards. Dozens of people ran in all directions, a few of them shrieking. Oh fuck—was that woman bleeding from the arm? Janine's heart began to pound harder. An arrow on a board pointed to the Resurrection Lab on her right. She pressed the accelerator. A fork in the road appeared. At its end sat a flat, grey building. That must be the one. She steered towards it, fast.

A man rushed out in front of her.

Janine registered a red beard and hoodie in the split-second before she wrenched the wheel and stamped on the brake. Tyres screeched. The man streaked past her windows in a blur. A median strip, arranged into a grassed hillock, loomed ahead. Too close, too late.

The car hit, bucked, and flipped.

She felt weightless for the briefest of moments.

Bang. The airbag thumped against her face, stunning her, starring her vision.

The car landed, hard, the impact shuddering through every bone. Slewing, sliding, scraping along the asphalt, the car finally ground to a halt. Sounds came back after a time. Dazed, Janine opened her eyes, blinked.

"Zeus?" she croaked. "*Heil*?" Unharmed?

He responded with the quick, short bark that meant *yes*.

The airbag had already deflated. Janine's nose hurt. She dabbed at her nostrils. Blood. And some kind of white powder, presumably from the deployed airbag.

It took a few seconds to get her bearings.

The car was lying on its side. The passenger window framed the grey and cloudy sky, while her head rested against the driver's window on the ground. The tempered safety glass had shattered. Any cuts? She passed both hands through her short brown hair. No. Fractures? Hastily, she palpated her jaw, her arms, thighs, moved her head around on her neck, flexed her feet. No. Apart from a sore nose, she appeared to be uninjured.

Jets of steam fired out from the bonnet.

Fuck. How much would this cost to repair?

Perhaps the accident would be covered on Victoria Police's vehicle insurance, even though it was Janine's personal car and the accident had technically occurred after-hours. By God, Harvey had better pick up the tab. And this would require a shitload of paperwork too. *Fuck.* Oh, and typically, no sign of the bearded, hoodie-wearing man who had run in front of her and caused this prang. Good old Joe Citizen. Never failing to shit himself in a crisis. Fuming, she unclipped her seatbelt.

"Okay," she said. "Let's figure a way out of here."

Zeus barked. Loud and long, repeatedly, an assault on Janine's ears.

What the hell? He never barked like this. Frantic, like an untrained dog. *Never.*

Could he be hurt? Janine looked back into the cargo area. Zeus, snarling, hackles raised, caramel eyes glittering, was fixated on something outside the car. Janine followed his gaze through the windscreen.

By the car bonnet stood a creature she didn't recognise.

A massive beast. A giant. Some kind of diabolic cross between a wolf and a big cat, a black-eyed bastard with a jaw that hung open to show nothing but canines, no molars. No molars? A shiver moved down Janine's back.

Tasmanian tiger…

Resurrection Lab…

She put two and two together. Got four.

The animal was an unholy concoction, an experiment, the handiwork of a mad scientist. Its eyes were as black as coal, unfathomable, yet it was looking at her, Janine had no doubt. Looking straight at her. *Hell hound.* Ordinarily, she didn't believe in demons, yet this abomination was almost enough to change her mind. Blood soaked the fur on its muzzle and face—blood from how many victims?

Distracted by something, the tiger glanced away and howled. The low, resonant and otherworldly note sent goose flesh prickling along Janine's arms. The tiger loped off. Oh God, it was *chasing* someone, a girl with long hair, and in any moment, it would catch her.

Galvanised, Janine hauled her legs up and over the steering wheel and placed both booted feet against the windscreen. The glass had already cracked. Three or four good kicks punched it out. She climbed out of the shattered windscreen and scanned the area.

Where was the tiger? Long gone. She couldn't see the girl it had been chasing either. Hopefully, the girl had got away.

Janine hurried to the back of the car. The gate had buckled somewhat in the crash, but she managed to wrench it open. Zeus hopped down and stood patiently, waiting. Janine grabbed his stab-resistant vest with its fluorescent blue POLICE decal and strapped it on him.

"Good boy," she murmured, running her hands over his head and shoulders, double-checking for any injury. No, he was okay. "*Bereit zu arbeiten?*" she added. Ready to work?

His tight muscles, stiffened tail, and closed mouth replied: *You bet your arse I'm ready.*

Now, Janine had to find her contact, the professor. What was the name? Rosie something-or-another. Janine looked about, spotted the Resurrection Lab, and ran towards it, holding the leash. Zeus trotted close at her heel.

A woman stood on the forecourt.

She had on a white lab coat.

Surely, that must be Rosie. She brandished a long pole in one hand. The automatic doors behind her were smashed. Perhaps the tigers had run through them to escape. As Janine approached, the woman began to wave madly, bouncing up and down on her toes as if Janine wouldn't be able to spot her. Rosie was old, wore glasses, her face red and tight with anxiety.

"You the professor?" Janine called.

"Yes, yes! Thank goodness you're here!"

***

Glenn, holding the jab stick upright in one fist, hurried along Centre Road towards the library. T1, T2 and T4 were nowhere in sight. There was, however, a flood of students racing towards him, away from the food court plaza and past the library. Glenn broke into a jog. Soon, he was going against the flow. The terrified crowd ran by him, unseeing.

A young man with acne and a hair-bun slowed to yell, "Hey, turn around! Mad dogs!"

"I know," Glenn said, continuing forward. "Thanks."

"You fucking idiot!" the man shrieked, already in the distance. "Run away! Run!"

And yeah, perhaps Glenn *was* being a fucking idiot. What did he hope to achieve with a single jab stick? He had given the other to Rosie. The silly old dear had refused to hide in an office like the rest of the staff. No, she was also going to hunt the tigers—with a mop handle. Naturally, he'd given her the second jab stick. Who wouldn't have done the same?

Upon reflection, however, it was a dumb move.

How many times had she deployed a stick? Twice? Would she know how to refill the syringe? Remember to pull the cocking lever first, rotate the safety cuff? Standing over Bill De Vries's corpse, with three tigers loose on campus, there hadn't been time to show her the steps—or so it had seemed. Glenn contemplated returning to the lab. Rosie would be a sitting duck. Yet so was everyone else on campus. And they didn't have defence weapons.

No. There could be no turning back.

Slowing his pace, Glenn began to walk by the glass front of the library. Dozens of scared faces showed through the tinted windows. The door cracked open. Betty, one of the librarians, stuck her head out and made a frantic beckoning gesture with her whole hand.

"Glenn," she said, "Hurry, come in where it's safe."

"Nah, I'm after the tigers."

"Tigers?" she said, mystified. "Those giant wolves are *tigers*?"

"Get back inside."

He kept on towards the food court plaza, glancing behind him every few steps. The fleeing crowd had thinned out. Students and staff must be either indoors or in vehicles.

"Wait!" Betty called. "Glenn, come back. You'll get hurt!"

Probably, he thought, and his guts tightened into a knot. But who else could take the risk? No one on campus was more qualified. His thoughts flicked to his wife, his kids.

Aw, shit. He should have *never* have taken this job.

Cloning the tigers in secret had *never* sat well with him.

Oh sure, the university dean and a few other knobs were aware of the program and had signed non-disclosure agreements just like Glenn. But to the rest of the world, the Resurrection Lab was trying to save the Tasmanian devil. A weird type of transmissible cancer was racing through the devil population on the island state of Tasmania. First noticed in 1996, the infection destroyed the animal's face—ate the tissues away, in fact, particularly around the mouth—and killed it, usually by starvation. Devil Facial Tumour Disease had wiped out about half the population so far. Extinction loomed. When Glenn had applied for the job at the Resurrection Lab all those years ago, he thought he'd be caring for Tassie devils, helping to find the cause of DFTD, the cure.

"Congratulations, you've got the job," Rosie had said at the end of the interview.

He had stood up, offered his hand to shake. "Beauty, thanks."

"Just a moment," she had said, raising her forefinger. "One more thing. My apologies. You'll need to sign this non-disclosure agreement before we go any further."

Sure, he'd signed it. So what? Plenty of places wanted to keep their techniques secret.

But after Rosie had explained the Thylacine De-Extinction Program to him, Glenn had almost walked away. Money spent chasing scientific pipe dreams should be invested in conservation instead. Endangered species took priority over extinct ones. Anybody with half a brain would agree. What about the right of the Tasmanian devil to live on? Or, for that matter, the right of the northern hairy-nosed wombat? Mountain pygmy possum? Western swamp tortoise? There were so many, many native Australian species, all deserving of help, all on the brink of disappearing forever, that ought to get the funding.

And the cloning process? Shit. Even when humanely practised, it still counted as vivisection. In the case of Tassie tigers, how many devils and red kangaroos—and clones—would have to suffer before a passable tiger litter could be produced?

The ethics bothered him then, when he had signed on for the job, and they had kept bothering him.

But Pam liked having babies. Dad needed expensive care in a specialised nursing home after getting dementia. And little brother Travis, drowning in debt from his gambling problem… But no, more than the generous pay cheque every week, Glenn had formed an attachment with the lab animals. Privately, telling no one else, he had named the Tassie devils, the red roos, the tigers. He gave each one the very best of care. Didn't trust anyone else to do it right. No one else *could* do it right. That's why he had stayed.

A flurry of cold winter rain hit Glenn's face, breaking his reverie.

Panicked, he spun around three-sixty degrees, saw an empty campus. Relief made him tremble. Fucking hell. What about situational awareness? His aunty—if she were alive to see him—would be kicking his arse right about now. *Don't ever turn your back* had been her mantra. The crocodiles on Aunty June's farm had been crafty bastards, always waiting for an opportunity. Still as statues, yet capable of lurching at speed if they felt like it.

Right now, Glenn either picked up his game or risked an ambush.

Focus.

He paused, collected himself, looked around again.

Quiet. So quiet.

A rumble of thunder sounded.

The sudden urge to pee was a sign of fear, and he ignored it. Hefting the jab stick to shoulder height, wielding it like a javelin, Glenn advanced towards the food court plaza. There, he stopped.

Deserted.

The central square was gravelled with fine white stones that needed constant raking. Slap-bang in the middle sat a giant metal sculpture of an emu. Park benches marked out the periphery. Glenn tightened his grip on the jab stick. A dozen eateries bordered the square: vegan, vegetarian, sandwich, salad. The odd-man-out was the stationery store, named "Paper." Turning slowly, very slowly, Glenn checked the windows. No faces showed.

A few doors stood open. Any of those shops might contain a tiger.

Or two.

Or all three.

Shit, if only he had his mobile. He would call Pam, let her know what was going on, tell her how much he loved her and all their kids—five so far (including a set of triplets), and one more in Pam's belly. But the greenies had stolen his phone. It was in Hannah's backpack, trapped behind bars in T6's cage. Pam might end up widowed. He might not have a chance to say goodbye. And the last thing he'd said to her that morning? *Don't forget to grab me a few tinnies while you're down at Woollies, darl.* Not exactly romantic.

Stop it, Glenn thought. *Stop shitting yourself.*

He would check the food court, one shop at a time.

On tiptoe, he advanced. His palms sweated heavily inside the cut-resistant gloves. Clouds were turning deep grey. A storm threatened. Pam's face again came to mind. *Jeez, I'm acting like the clichéd soldier in a Hollywood war film,* he thought, *mooning over a picture of my sweetheart before copping a bullet to the scone.*

He chuckled a little at that. Tried to chuckle, anyway.

7

Rosie led the policewoman, Janine O'Connell, and her tracker dog, Zeus, along the hallway of the Resurrection Lab towards the animal enclosure. O'Connell took long, rangy strides. Rosie had to scurry to keep up. And this blasted jab stick was so darned *heavy*.

"Officer, your nose is bleeding," Rosie said.

"I know," O'Connell said. "So, thylacines, huh?"

"Yes." Rosie hesitated. "More or less."

"More or less? You've got that right. I saw one of them outside. It was a freak."

Rosie felt herself blush. "De-extinction is not an exact science. Not yet."

"Maybe not ever."

"I can assure you we're almost there."

O'Connell sneered. "Really? Then you ought to quit while you still can."

Rosie clamped her lips. The prejudice, the unfounded, uneducated, superstitious *prejudice* that her field of study attracted made her blood boil. The typical stupid person always assumed the worst. Had only the limited intellectual capacity, the stunted imagination, to assume the worst. Stupid people had called Rosie derogatory nicknames—usually Dr Frankenstein—both to her face and behind her back for years. But how to change stupid people's minds? When they were afraid of life-saving vaccines, thought "Big Pharma" was hiding a one-size-fits-all cancer cure, trusted that an inert vial of "medicine" diluted down to nothing but pure water would have any kind of effect?

With the clench of a fist, Rosie forced her pet peeve out of mind. Tragedies had occurred, *crimes* had occurred, and must be dealt with promptly by the proper authorities.

"Just to warn you," she said, "we have two dead bodies in the enclosure."

"Dead bodies don't bother me."

"There was another by the entry, but an ambulance came and took him away."

O'Connell didn't reply. Hell's bells, this woman could walk *fast*.

A policeman stood by the enclosure door. O'Connell took out her badge. He waved her inside. O'Connell and Zeus went in first, leaving Rosie to trail behind. Once again, she had to scurry to catch up. Tasmanian devils yowled. Perhaps they were hungry. Where could Glenn be? Please God, let him be all right. She shouldn't have taken one of his jab sticks. Glenn was out on campus, barely armed, and what had she been doing? Giving statements to officers, that's what. Hardly the necessity for a jab stick.

"Explain what happened," O'Connell said. "In a nutshell."

And now Rosie must give her statement *again*. At least she had it down pat.

"We had a meeting with executives about our funding. A trio of activists burst in with guns and opened the thylacine cages. The girl tried to pet a thylacine and was killed. Then another activist shot dead an executive, by mistake, I believe. The remaining two activists were mauled to death."

"And where are their bodies?"

"In the main laboratory. I can show you if you like."

"No need. That's another squad's responsibility. We're here to track the tigers."

Bill De Vries's assistant, Simon, lay where Llewellyn's bullet had felled him. He had turned a mottled grey colour, and the blood on his chest had thickened into a dark, set jelly. The sight upset Rosie's stomach. Two uniformed policemen stood, casually, near poor Simon. One was actually fooling with a mobile phone. Their cavalier attitude infuriated her. Why on earth weren't they *doing* something? Why weren't they out catching the thylacines?

O'Connell approached the two men, and said, "Oh, hey, Robbo."

The blond officer turned and grinned. "Oh, g'day, Janine. How ya doing?"

"It's my sixth hour of overtime after a full nightshift. How do you think I'm doing?"

He laughed. "Rugged. Janine, this is Mark."

They shook hands.

"Babysitting for Homicide?" Janine said.

"Yeah," Robbo said. "Hi there, Zeus, little buddy."

"He's working." O'Connell moved past them. To Rosie, she said, "How many thylacines are missing?"

"Three. In this last cage is the activist girl and the remains of T6, thylacine number six. These officers shot him dead. Glenn Hart, my animal handler, tranquillised and bound two others in the main laboratory. The officers shot them too. Right now, Glenn is out on campus, trying to find and decommission the remaining thylacines. He needs urgent help."

O'Connell stood at T6's open cage and gazed upon the carnage within, hands on hips, apparently unmoved. Blood and brain matter spattered the walls. The activist, Hannah, looked human from the neck down. From the neck up, she was a gory, flattened slop of hair, splintered bone, and clots. Rosie swallowed the rising tide of bile and glanced away.

"Do the tigers hunt in a pack?" O'Connell said.

"What? Oh, no one knows for sure. Historical records are scanty. Sometimes they hunted alone. Other times, they hunted in family groups."

O'Connell sighed. "Not real Tassie tigers. *Your* tigers. Will they run in a pack?"

Good question. Rosie had no idea. The litter had been separated, one to a cage, their entire lives. Perplexity must have shown on Rosie's face, since O'Connell rolled her eyes.

"Okay," she said, "is there a tiger more dominant than the others?"

"Yes. T1. The first-born."

"Show us his cage."

Rosie pointed.

O'Connell entered T1's cage with Zeus by her side. Picking up a handful of bedding straw, she proffered it to the dog and said, "*Ziel.*"

"What does that mean?" Rosie said, as the dog sniffed deeply, burying its muzzle.

"It's German for 'target.' I'm asking Zeus to track T1."

"But they're clones. Brothers with identical genes. They'll smell alike."

"No, they won't. Tracker dogs can tell the difference."

"Really?"

"Yeah, really. Even when the subjects live in the same place and eat the same food."

Of course, Rosie thought. It made sense. In nature, genes could be expressed differently between identical siblings. So why not in clones? The thylacines, despite sharing the same genome, had subtle variations in markings. For example, T1 had thicker swipes of white fur beneath his eyes, much more pronounced than the others. In humans, monozygotic siblings might have different skin freckling; sometimes, different fingerprints. Why shouldn't the thylacine clones each have a unique scent? Zeus would track T1 into a corner, and O'Connell would shoot to kill. Except... O'Connell's uniform lacked the utility belt.

Good gracious, where was her *gun*? Vexed, Rosie clamped her lips. This wouldn't do.

"Shouldn't you be armed?" she said.

"My kit's back at the squad room. Zeus and I were heading home when we got the call."

"Here, take this." Rosie pulled Llewellyn's gun from her lab coat. "It's not loaded, unfortunately. Perhaps your policeman friend could spare a few bullets."

***

Zeus snuffled through the building via a winding route—zigzagging the corridor in and out of offices—yet he inexorably headed towards the smashed glass doors at the entrance. Janine walked behind him, the grip of the leash in one hand. The copper guarding the door nodded to her on her way out, and she returned the gesture.

The vast, sprawling campus had countless places for the tigers to hide.

At least she now had a gun, an M&P .40 calibre Smith & Wesson semi-automatic pistol, loaded with a full magazine and a spare in her pocket thanks to Robbo and his partner, Mark. Come to think of it, however, she hadn't asked the professor a single question about the gun. Whose was it? Where did the professor get it? Janine didn't know. Uh oh, sloppy police work, but she couldn't do anything about that right now. Zeus, nose down, had already led her through the broken glass across the forecourt and down the steps.

Janine phoned the sergeant, Harvey Nussbaum. He answered on the second ring.

"I need back-up," Janine said. "We've got three tigers at large. I can only track one."

"Hang fire. You'll have reinforcements within half an hour, maybe forty minutes."

The winter clouds had knitted together, deepened into a dark blue-grey, hunkering near the ground. Goddamn. Tracker dogs couldn't work in the rain. Water rinsed away the scent. Zeus tugged on the leash. Janine lengthened her stride into a jog.

"Harvey, for Christ's sake, hurry up," she said. "Once it rains, we're fucked."

Without waiting for a reply, she hung up and pocketed the phone. The wind felt icy. She should have remembered to grab her coat from the car. Too bad. She swapped the leash to her left hand, and took the gun from her waistband. Zeus would find T1. With any luck, the tigers would be in a pack, and *bang bang bang*, job done, everybody could go home. Janine was a good shot. At the refresher courses she attended every few months, she consistently scored high, particularly on the twenty-five-metre range.

She checked the signposts. Currently, they were jogging along Harrison Drive towards the Allen James Hall. Movement caught her eye. In the distance, at the far end of Centre Road, crawled a patrol car, the white sedan with its blue chequered decal standing out like dog's balls against the lush greenery of the hills beyond—

Realisation hit her.

Oh, *fuck* no.

Fraser University backed onto the Yarra Ranges National Park.

A wild forest.

Mountain ash forest and cool temperate rainforest, to be precise, with few roads and limited access. If the tigers escaped into those ranges, there would be no catching them. Did the university have a rear fence? Janine had no idea. But even if there *was* a rear fence, what good would it serve? The campus roads weren't gated. The tigers could find a dozen different ways out of here without breaking a sweat.

Janine tucked the gun into her waistband to call Harvey.

"Send more cars," she told him. "Lots more. We need to secure the perimeter and keep the tigers on site. Once they're in the forest, they're gone for good."

"Look, I'm doing the best I can."

She hung up. Zeus was keeping a regular pace, sometimes dropping his nose to the ground. They veered off Harrison Drive onto a median strip some ten metres wide. Then he began looping around in large, pointless circles. No, he hadn't lost the scent—he was trained to sit down if that happened. This must have been a scene of butchery, where T1 had encountered a group of students and charged at random. And yep, there was the tell-tale blood on the kerb, a few splashes on the grass. No victims in sight, however. Janine remembered her first aid kit, stashed in the glove box of her car, and frowned. After the prang, she should have taken a few moments to clear her head and get organised. But the sight of that tiger... Christ. That freakish thing had unnerved her, thrown her off—

A bell sounded from hidden speakers, and she startled.

"Attention staff and students," said a disembodied female voice, the strain evident in the quick speech, high pitch, fast breathing. "Dangerous animals are still loose on campus. Stay indoors. If you are outside, head to the nearest building immediately. Do *not* try to leave in your car. There have been attacks in and around the car parks. Please, all staff and students should be inside. Stay calm. The police are here."

Zeus crossed the median and started along Brooke Road. According to the signpost, they were heading towards the Institute for Molecular Biology. Must be that ugly orange brick building. Shit, Janine's calves were getting tight, loaded down with lactic acid. Too much jogging on top of the kilometres she'd already run last night during her shift. A dull headache started up. She exhaled a few times, hard, forcing fresh air into her lungs. Fatigued or not, she had better keep her mind on the job.

They passed a side street. Janine glanced down it. A divisional van cruised past. *Come on, Harvey,* she thought. Pull your bloody finger out. Two cop cars are not nearly enough.

Zeus led her past the giant building that housed the molecular biology department. On the other side of the road beyond a lawn sat a garish, multi-coloured building that brought to mind a Rubik's cube. Janine shook her head. No sense of continuity in the architecture. Ten different designers must have cobbled this place together with one common aim: to make sure no building resembled another. Well, they had succeeded. The campus looked like shit.

A horn tooted. Behind her was a van. She hadn't heard its approach over the gusting wind.

"*Warten*," she told Zeus, and he obediently stopped to wait.

The van had ANIMAL CONTROL plastered all over it. The man sitting in the passenger side poked his head out the open window and waved.

"G'day," he said. "You know which way we ought to go?"

"You want the Resurrection Lab. Back up to the last intersection and take the turn-off. Talk to the professor there. Her name's Rosie."

"Cheers," he said.

The van's engine whined as the driver reversed it with a heavy foot.

"You need to call out more vans," Janine shouted. "As many as you've got."

"On their way," the passenger called.

Good luck, she thought. Hopefully, they had more than just nets and grab poles, but she doubted it.

"*Gehen*," she said, and Zeus took off again.

They passed the molecular biology institute, cut through a garden bed filled with acacias, and came out on another road, this one called Sullivan Crescent. Janine checked the signs. Western Lecture Centre coming up on the left, Fraser University Credit Centre on the right, dead ahead a stretch of parkland amidst the asphalt, thickly planted with mature eucalyptus trees. Zeus barked twice, his warning signal. Janine's heart rate accelerated.

What was that lying on the grass?

Her hand tightened on the pistol. She broke into a run.

It was a person, lying supine, limbs flung out at careless angles.

By the time Janine reached the victim's side, Zeus was growling. The victim, little more than a boy, perhaps eighteen years old, had a meagre scattering of stray hairs on his chin, and his throat ripped out. Ripped clean out. Trachea gone. Oesophagus, thyroid, jugulars, and carotids gone. Janine could see right through to the neck bones. His corpse lay in a pool of dark, congealing blood.

Christ almighty.

And the hapless kid's face. A look of surprise, astonishment. He must have died even as he wondered what the hell was going on.

Janine's perusal took less than a moment. Zeus's growls turned into frantic barks. Adrenaline shot through Janine's limbs. She heard the rustling of leaves, the breaking of branches, and understood what was about to happen in a split-second. She had one final thought—*how the fuck did it climb a tree when it has paws like a dog?*—before the tiger dropped on her.

A glimpse of short golden fur, a huge clawed foot, an open mouth full of teeth.

No time to scream.

The tiger knocked her flat, punched the air out of her, and broke her wrist as the gun barrel impacted the ground and twisted her hand too far sideways. A flare of agonising pain. She tasted grass, dirt, panic. Hot breath fanned across the nape of her neck. Snapping teeth pulled out hanks of hair. She kicked, struggled.

Oh God, she would end up like the boy next to her.

Worse, like the animal activist with her head chewed off.

She had to buck this monster, free her gun and shoot before it could bite. No, *fuck*, she couldn't move. The tiger was too heavy. Heavy as a sandbag, heavy enough to suffocate her with its weight. She couldn't breathe. *I don't want to die.* But this was it. The End.

Unbelievable.

Death by lab freak. How fucking *ridiculous* is that?

Oh no, oh damn, this would kill her parents. Break their hearts.

Make a run for it, Zeus. *Run.*

Zeus hadn't stopped barking. The tiger, lumbering its paws over her back, buttocks and legs, its stupendous weight creaking her ribs and bruising her flesh, answered with an eerie, reptilian hiss. Then its weight lifted. Gasping, Janine raised her head.

The animals were facing off.

Zeus was big for a German Shepherd—seventy centimetres tall at the withers, forty-three kilos in weight—but he resembled a puppy next to this behemoth. The tiger stood at least twice Zeus's height. And its weight? One hundred and twenty kilos, easy. Maybe more. The fur was so short that every ripple and flex of muscle stood out in bas-relief. Janine could even see the veins. If a wolf ate steroids for breakfast and weight-trained three hours a day, this is what the bastard would look like. Drying blood masked the tiger's face, right up to its ears, as if the tiger had dunked its head into a bucket of gore. How many people had this freak wounded or killed? Janine rolled onto her side, wincing.

Shoot the fucking thing. She had to shoot it *now*.

Ears back, nose wrinkled, body tensed, Zeus leapt from foot to foot, bobbing and weaving, a boxer looking for an opening. *No.* If he attacked, he would die. But wait, the tiger seemed taken aback, perplexed. Almost frightened. It held its body close to the ground and cocked its head from side to side, whining.

So, the fucker had never seen a dog before.

Janine struggled to her knees. With a broken wrist, the fingers of her right hand refused to work. She took the gun into her left hand. It felt awkward, unnatural. Clumsily, she thumbed off the safety, aimed, pulled the trigger.

Crack.

At the loud noise, the tiger whipped its giant head around and fixed her with blackened eyes the size of fucking baseballs. Yet it hadn't reacted as if hurt, hadn't yelped or flinched.

Jesus Christ. Had she *missed*?

She fired again.

Another miss. How? The tiger stood *right there*. Fuck, her hand must be shaking.

Zeus ducked and darted at the monster, snarling, teeth bared, trying to draw its ire away from her. And his ploy worked. The tiger yawned open those terrible jaws, wide, wide like an opening book, and lunged at Zeus. Janine's imagination skipped ahead, saw her K9 partner crushed and lifeless, saw herself at home, crying, packing away his kennel, hiding his food and water bowls in the garage so she wouldn't be reminded of him, and she narrowed her focus to a goddamned laser point and held the gun straight out at arm's length.

Janine's third shot sank into the tiger's hip.

The tiger sprang into the air, all four feet simultaneously off the ground, bounding a good two metres straight up. Hell on wheels, Janine thought in amazement, it can jump like a fucking *kangaroo*. When it landed, it took off at speed, limping on the injured leg.

Janine fired after it, again and again, but the tiger didn't cry out, falter or stumble, not once. Fuck. Six more shots equalling six more misses. The tiger kept running. Its back legs were comparatively short, so it ran like a hyena. But what a strange tail. Not like that of a dog or cat, but of a kangaroo. The tiger raced behind the Western Lecture Centre and out of sight.

Janine sat back, dropped her arm to her side, panting.

Well, what do you know? This was the first time she had ever fired a gun in the line of duty—using her off-hand, no less—and she had *sucked*. Every other time had been while training at the Academy or during refresher courses at the shooting range. Lesson learned. Being an expert marksman against a motionless paper target is in no way indicative of your performance in the field. An instructor had told her that once. She'd doubted him then, but now? Yep, duly noted.

She let go of the gun. Wiped the dirt and grass from her mouth. All the various pains in her body came to her attention at once. Zeus trotted over, concern in his intelligent eyes. He licked her cheek.

"Good boy," she murmured, pressing her face into his shoulder, gripping his fur in her good hand. She was trembling. So was he. "You're a good boy, aren't you? Yes, you are."

After a moment, she pulled away to inspect her wrist. The fall must have concertinaed the bones, since her wrist now had a hump. God, it hurt like blazes. All right, think, how many times had she fired the gun? About nine times, she was pretty sure. So, one bullet left for the chamber. Clumsily, she ejected the magazine and inserted the other, one-handed. Then she called Harvey.

"I don't know how much good I'm going to be," she told him. "A tiger attacked me and I broke my wrist."

"You okay apart from that?"

"I think so." Her ribs hurt but she could still breathe. That must mean they were intact.

"All right," Harvey said. "Go, get out of there. Can you still drive?"

"What? No, I just meant I need more coppers here ASAP."

"You're not carrying on with the trail, are you? With a knackered arm?"

"Of course I am," she said, and her gaze stole over the grass to the dead boy, lying nearby with his throat gone, and she hung up.

8

Glenn decided to check the shops in an orderly fashion.

The first shop with an open door happened to be Paper, which sold stationery. He approached, jab stick propped at his shoulder. His boots crunched on stray pieces of white gravel. The groundskeepers raked here daily, sure, but the constant passage of students walking over the central square kicked and scattered gravel all over the surrounding footpaths. Years ago, the central square had featured grass, also no match against pedestrian traffic. Bricks, cobblestones or tiles should have replaced the grass. What kind of drongo chooses *loose gravel*?

Focus.

He paused at the doorway of Paper. Okay, someone had turned off the lights. Glenn reached around with his free hand and groped at the wall until he found the switch. Banks of overhead fluorescent tubes winked and ticked, causing a momentary strobing effect. Glenn took a sharp breath.

Tiger.

The lights blinked and stayed on. No, wait, not a tiger. The silhouette belonged to a cut-out of a cartoon wombat grinning over a display of pens: twelve-packs of ballpoints on sale for $5.00 each. Glenn stepped inside and closed the door behind him.

Nowhere for a tiger to hide. Too much open space. Goods were displayed along shelves built into the walls, and in bins arranged in a line down the middle of the shop. The place smelled like plastic binders, markers, glue-sticks. No distinctive scent of the Tassie tiger—a musky, yeasty, shitty combination—and Glenn blew out his breath. *Safe*.

However, there was a toilet in back, the door ajar. He approached with a light tread.

Blood on the floor.

Huge gobs of blood.

He stopped. What was that noise? Soft, muffled. It sounded like crying. Tigers had a range of vocalisations, could sound like parrots, snakes, dingoes, cats, abandoned babies…

"Hello?" Glenn said.

"We're in here!"

He shoved open the door. On the tiled floor sat two women, one middle-aged and fleshy, the other with a bloody towel wrapped around her lower leg. Her foot stuck out on an unnatural angle, her ankle obviously broken. A tiger must have snapped her bones in one bite.

Glenn closed the door and propped the jab stick against the wall.

"How bad is it?" he said, dropping to his knees.

Dazed, the middle-aged women made as if to remove the towel. Glenn stopped her.

"No, don't," he said. "You'll start the wounds bleeding again. Put more pressure on it."

The injured woman turned her glazed eyes towards him, and murmured, "Demon dog."

Glenn looked about the bathroom and spotted a shelf with a stack of folded hand towels. Grabbing one, he wrapped it around the woman's leg on top of the existing towel, and gently secured the lot with four, five, six revolutions of duct tape.

"That ought to do it," he said. "Why did you leave the dunny door open?"

"What?" said the older woman.

"The tiger could have come back and finished you both."

"Demon dog." The injured woman began to cry again. "Demon dog. *Demon dog!*"

Glenn stood up. "Can one of youse lend me a phone?"

"What?"

"A phone, a mobile."

The older woman gaped blankly while the other wept. Forget it. Even if he found their mobiles—no doubt both handbags were stashed behind the front counter—these sheilas weren't *compos mentis* enough to unlock them.

"Stay here," he said, and picked up the jab stick.

Closing the door behind him, he hurried to the front of the store. The counter had a monitor, keyboard, mouse, EFTPOS facility. And a landline, thank God.

He snatched up the handset, rang home.

Got the answering machine.

Shit.

He hung up, called Pam's mobile. Straight to voicemail.

For a second, he contemplated hanging up again. What could he possibly say into a machine at a time like this? He noticed blood on his glove. Blood from the woman holed up in the dunny back there, losing her mind. The voicemail beeped. He cleared his throat.

"Darl?" he said. "Look, there's trouble at work. I'm trying to fix things. Dunno how it'll pan out." He paused as tears pricked his eyes. "Thanks for being my missus, all right?"

He disconnected, wiped at his face with the back of his forearm. The toilet door flung open. There stood the older woman, mouth contorted into a tense, panicked grimace.

"Don't go," she said.

"I have to."

"No. You don't."

Yeah, she had a point. Why not stay? The exterior door of Paper was shut. Tigers couldn't get in. He should wait out this crisis in safety. Besides, he'd seen a cop car on his way over to the food court plaza. Heard sirens in the distance. And gunshots? No need to be a hero. Not with Pam and the kids depending on him.

Yet the bitten woman just wouldn't stop crying.

He could hear her, sobbing and snivelling. There would be other vulnerable people like her on campus, people in danger, people Glenn could save. Crikey, he had a moral responsibility to act. He was the animal handler, wasn't he? Too right. Only *he* knew the tigers. To everybody else they were… demon dogs.

"Get back inside and shut the door," he said.

"Please don't leave us."

"I'll send help, all right? Just shut the door."

The injured woman, unseen, began wailing and keening.

"I swear on my Aunty June's grave," he said, taking up the jab stick and moving out from behind the counter, "that Tassie tigers can't turn door handles. I swear it."

The older woman nodded, retreated, and pulled the toilet door closed.

Glenn went to the glass front of Paper and took a long time inspecting the food court plaza. That bloody emu statue in the middle of the gravelled square... At best, the statue looked like a flamingo. Before break-up every year, idiots wrapped it in dunny paper.

The door handle felt cold through his gloves, felt good against his sweating fingers. He glanced at the landline. Maybe he should try Pam again. The muffled sobs of the injured woman made him step outside.

The wind had a bite to it. Nipped at his nose. Raised the hairs on his bare legs. Trying to keep quiet, treading softly to avoid scraping on stray chunks of gravel, he advanced towards the next shop with an open door: a café named Full Fork Eatery. Not a bad place, actually. Had a pretty good chicken and mushroom pie, which Pam reckoned was a *vol au vent*, not a pie, as it didn't have a pastry lid. *Shit*, he thought, hesitating. He should go back to Paper and try calling the missus again. That ambiguous message he'd left on her voicemail would distress her. Then he saw the tiger.

His skin clenched and pin-prickled up the back of his neck.

The tiger stood on the opposite side of the square, watching with sombre eyes and a closed mouth. Drying blood soaked the fur on its face. Not its own blood, for there were no lacerations. Human blood. The bent tip of one ear identified the tiger as Droopy—thylacine number four, T4. Meeker than his brothers. Sometimes Droopy liked to press against the bars of his cage and allow his disfigured ear to be scratched, but only for a few seconds.

"G'day, Droopy. Hey, little mate. Time to go home."

Last chance. Last chance to run and hide. Glenn tightened his grip on the jab stick.

Droopy looked away and trotted along the concrete path on the other side of the square, back leg dragging. The tiger seemed purposeful, as if he had a destination in mind. Glenn, sweat trickling from his hairline despite the cold wind, did nothing but observe. It was a serious injury, for sure.

A bell sounded from speakers. "All staff and students are to remain inside," implored the university secretary over the PA. "Do not go outside. I repeat: do *not* go outside."

Droopy stopped walking and hung his head, panting. Then he sat down in the manner reminiscent of a dog: sideways, on one bum cheek. He fixed Glenn with sad, wet eyes. Yeah, he was badly injured, all right. Blood pumped down his right leg and pooled on the concrete.

"Hey, what happened? How'd you get hurt?"

Probably shot by a copper. Despite the heavy bleeding, the wound itself—high on the thigh near the hip joint—appeared small and neat.

Droopy whined, stood up on all fours with difficulty, and headed towards the open door of the Cravetarian restaurant. Glenn started after him. Admittedly, they had only interacted through the bars of a cage, yet he fed Droopy twice per day. Wasn't "cupboard love" a valid connection between humans and animals? And the talking, the care, the familiarity of Glenn's presence day after day, month after month… wasn't that worth something to an animal, even a fucked-up synthetic one created in a petri dish?

Droopy's back legs wobbled and he sat down again.

Glenn halted. Studied the body language. Droopy gazed imploringly with limpid eyes.

"You want help? Because I'm here for you, little mate. I'm here."

Yet Droopy must recognise the jab stick. He had been stuck plenty of times; for medical check-ups, dental care, the taking of blood samples. None of the tigers liked the jab stick. Glenn took it off his shoulder and tried to hide it behind his body.

"Come on over here. Okay? Come on over," he said, making kissing noises like he did when brandishing a chicken above a tiger's slavering jaws, the bird flapping and squawking.

Droopy got up and staggered onwards, leaving a spattered trail of blood in his wake. He limped inside the restaurant. Glenn broke into a jog, cutting across the gravel.

Unlike Paper, Cravetarian had the lights on.

Giant poster-boards of vegetables decorated the walls: capsicums, tomatoes, eggplants. A dozen or so tables, each set with four places. Abandoned meals on most of the tables. Salads. Soup and rolls. Eggs on toast. Scattered chairs, a few lying on the floor. Blood here and there.

At the far end of the restaurant sat Droopy.

Mouth still closed, ears relaxed. Docile. No threat display. Glenn advanced.

"Come on, little mate. Come on over and see what I've got for you."

He lowered the jab stick to hip height, trying to hold it casually. Next, the tricky part. The poke of the injection itself would give Droopy a fright. Secondly, the mixture of ketamine and diazepam would provoke a few moments of frenzied, disorganised activity. Glenn needed to use the jab stick quickly and then leap back out of harm's way. Droopy might hurt him, even without meaning to, by jumping and flailing around.

Droopy's head moved sideways. Glenn turned his gaze in the same direction.

Boomer—T4—moved out from behind the counter and stopped.

Well, fuck me dead, Glenn thought in surprise, as an intense shiver of fear quivered through him. An ambush. Droopy stood up on all fours—*with ease*—which meant the tiger must have feigned the severity of the gunshot wound in order to fool Glenn, to lure him into the restaurant. *Strewth.* How fucking smart were these animals? *Too smart, too smart...*

Motionless, sharing the same posture, the tigers stared with hard, unblinking eyes.

Glenn yelled the made-up word he used when exercising his authority: "Hep! *Hep!*" Always, the word made them cower, acquiesce. But not now. He pressed his back against the wall to keep both tigers in sight at the same time. The only sound in his ears was the chaotic drumming of his own heart.

Think.

What was the plan?

Okay, Droopy was injured. Boomer made more sense as a target. Then again, perhaps the smartest option would be to make a run for it, shut the door on his way out, trap the tigers inside the restaurant. Yes, that was it. That's what he would do. Adrenaline flooded Glenn's leg muscles, made his knees shake, his boots hammer against the floorboards. Getting ready to sprint, he looked towards the exit.

The pack leader, T1—Phoenix—stood in the doorway.

***

Dr Linda Chang, eyes red and swollen, sat at Glenn's desk, gnawing on her fingernails. Thank heavens, Rosie thought, the silly woman has stopped crying at last.

Striding into the office, Rosie said, "Feeling better?"

"Oh, I don't know. I suppose so."

"Good. Because I'm leaving you in charge."

Linda sat bolt upright and gasped as if slapped. "Me?"

"Yes, you. These policemen," she pointed at the officers standing by Simon's corpse, "have informed me that Homicide detectives will be here within the next three minutes. You are to wait at the front doors to greet them and bring them up to speed."

"But... but the front doors are *smashed*."

"Correct."

"What about the thylacines?"

"An armed policeman is out front. I'm quite sure he'll shoot any on sight."

Linda clapped a hand to her forehead and gazed around at the desktop, as if Glenn's diary, notepad, or feed brochures might suggest a plausible excuse. Annoyed, Rosie gave an exaggerated sigh and clucked her tongue.

"But the phone," Linda said. "Who's going to answer the phone?"

"I will advise Indigo to take your place. The council is sending over more dog-catchers. You'll need to brief everyone who comes to the building." Rosie took a notepad from her pocket. "Here are the names and numbers of the authorities you and Indigo are to liaise with and update, as required. Consider yourself the communications officer. Now, come along."

Rosie turned and went to leave the office.

"Wait." Linda stood up. "Where are *you* going?"

"Where do you think?" Rosie said, shaking the jab stick. "I'm not carrying this for decoration." She left the office and marched along the corridor towards the enclosure exit.

"Tell me you're not serious," Linda said, falling in beside her.

"Oh, my *word*, I'm serious."

"You can't capture a thylacine by yourself. You'll get hurt."

"Then so be it."

Linda grabbed her arm in a vice-like grip, bringing her to a standstill.

"Please let me go," Rosie said. "My mind is made up."

"None of this is your fault."

Rosie set her teeth and lifted her chin against a sudden pricking of tears. "Not my fault, perhaps, but certainly my responsibility." Pulling her arm free, she left the enclosure and headed towards the lunchroom.

"I can't let you do this," Linda said, trailing behind.

"Hah! And how do you intend to stop me? I'm carrying a loaded jab stick." At the lunchroom, Rosie flung open the door. Her huddled staff jumped as one and stared at her with frightened eyes. "Indigo, you are now under Linda's authority. Head to Glenn's office to man the phones and assist the policemen as they require."

"Yes, Professor Giuliani," Indigo said meekly, scrambling to her feet.

Rosie turned on her heel and headed down the hall. Cold, wintry air fanned in through the broken front doors. Voices behind her—*Where is she going? To catch a thylacine. Oh my God. That's ridiculous! Somebody ought to bring her back. Is she crazy?*—yet no one came after her and she didn't break her stride.

The policeman stationed at the front doors began, "Um, excuse me—?"

"Just do your job, if you wouldn't mind," she said, stomping across the broken glass.

"Ma'am, for your own safety, you need to stay inside."

"I'm well aware of that, thank you. I appreciate your concern."

She hurried down the steps. Which way should she go? The thylacines could be literally anywhere. She headed towards the biotechnology department, as good a place as any to begin her search. In the top pocket of her lab coat were three vials of tranquilliser; in the hip pocket, a roll of duct tape. How clever of Glenn to truss the sedated thylacines in such a manner. That young man could certainly think on his feet. A pang of anxiety tightened Rosie's throat.

Please God, let Glenn be okay.

With a toss of her head, she pushed aside the desire to pray. It was nothing but a reflex. In times of trouble, people fall back into habitual coping patterns, and she was no different.

Drizzle fell, softly, the spits of rain whisking and whirling on the breeze. Rosie glanced up. The clouds were busy wringing themselves into violent knots. Soon, it would be pouring. She should have brought an umbrella. Tough luck. It couldn't be helped.

Good *grief*, the jab stick was heavy. She swapped it to the other hand, tried hugging it against her stomach, then resting it behind her neck over both shoulders. Great care was required, however. The safety cuff was rotated to the "off" position. The slightest pressure at the business end would depress the plunger. Ten ccs of ketamine and diazepam? No thanks.

A line of police cars headed towards her on Centre Road. She pointed emphatically at the Resurrection Lab. The first car flashed its lights and turned as directed, the other cars following suit. Hopefully, Linda and Indigo would be up to the task.

She rounded the building that housed the biotechnology department and, on a whim, decided to head to the food court plaza. It was lunchtime after all, and she was hungry.

Goodness, she had never seen the campus so abandoned. A ghost town. Her heart was beating fast, so fast that it seemed to thrum like the wings of a hummingbird, but whether from fear or brisk walking, she couldn't tell.

Linda's words: *None of this is your fault.*

Then whose?

One could split as many hairs as one wanted. Perhaps blame Bill De Vries for breaking the non-disclosure agreement and inadvertently tipping off the activists, or blame the activists themselves for opening the cages. However, there would have been no cages to open if Rosie had not spent her life chasing the dream of bringing the thylacine back to life.

"Professor Giuliani!"

She startled and spun around. Neil, a campus security guard, ambled out of the laneway that ran behind a row of cafés. He was a heavy, thickset man with a receding hairline and a bristling monobrow.

"Gee, I'm sorry," he said. "I didn't mean to frighten you."

Rosie chuckled at herself and shook her head. "Oh, that's quite all right."

"Pretty spooky with no one about, hey?"

"Indeed." She looked at his hands, his utility belt. "A baton? That's it?"

He shrugged. "That's all the equipment we're allowed."

"No emergency cache of guns?"

He sniggered a laugh through his nose. "I wish."

"You ought to go inside."

"Speak for yourself. Don't worry about me, this baton is hard enough to crack a dog's noggin. So, what have you got there, a spear?"

A flash of movement by the nearest dumpster. The thylacine rose up behind Neil and wrapped its front paws around his neck.

Rosie screamed. Neil's eyes bulged. Dropping the baton, gurgling, he clawed at the headlock. The grip was too strong.

Good Lord, the thylacine was actually *strangling* him.

Rosie clenched the jab stick in both hands and lunged. The thylacine, balancing on tail and hind legs, nimbly darted out of reach, dangling Neil from its paws with the casual ease of a child hugging a rag doll. Oh, but Rosie had to take *extra* care. What if she stuck Neil by mistake? The high dose of the tranquilliser might kill him. Yet every moment she hesitated, Neil's face turned a darker shade of red.

She lunged again. And again, the thylacine sidestepped her attack.

"Damn you!" she screamed, her throat stripping raw.

Those huge, wet, dark eyes stared back. Inscrutable, unreadable, unearthly. Black sclerae, black irises, black pupils. The eyes of the Devil himself.

Neil's face had turned purple. His arms flopped as if boneless. Oh, dear God, the man was *dying* right in front of her. Rosie feinted to the animal's right. When it predictably jumped left, she stabbed it, hard, in the groin.

The thylacine reacted as if touched by live wires.

Dropping Neil, howling, it sprang high into the air and bounded in crazed circles. Rosie had no time to retreat. Its tail, thick as a man's arm, cracked across her shoulder and threw her to the ground. She landed heavily on the cobblestones. The jab stick rolled away. The thylacine, a whirling dervish, whipped and wailed so close to her face that she gagged on its strong, musty odour. No, no, no, *the dose was too small*. At any second, a foot would land on her head and split her skull.

Just as suddenly as it had begun, the thylacine's mad dance ended.

The creature fell in a messy, sprawling heap, drooling with its tongue out. Breath held, Rosie watched and waited. Blindly, the thylacine groped about the cobblestones with its four paws and lashing tail, trying in vain to stay upright. The lupine poise and elegance were gone. She saw the thylacine for what it really was: a bizarre creation from a bad fever dream; a godless, monstrous nightmare; a composite of gnashing teeth and long, snapping jaws. Its eyelids flickered. Those fiendish eyes rolled up into its head. The beast crashed sideways and began to snore.

Neil lay nearby on his back, motionless.

Rosie, her senses returning, crawled over to him.

"Oh, my Lord," she gasped. "Neil? Can you hear me? Neil?"

No reply. Was he unconscious? *Dead?* His face looked grey. She grabbed the lapels of his shirt and shook him with all her strength. His flabby cheeks and jowls wobbled.

"Answer me," she roared. "Neil!"

He began coughing. Rosie let him go and sagged with relief. *Oh, Blessed Virgin Mary*, she thought, fighting back tears. *Who can worthily give you the just dues of praise and thanksgiving, you, who by the wondrous assent of your will, rescued a fallen world?*

"Fucking hell," Neil croaked, and he rolled over and spat.

"I'm glad you're all right. Now go indoors and stay there."

She crawled towards the thylacine, the cobblestones digging into her knees and palms.

Neil sat up and flinched. "What the fuck *is* that thing?"

"I'm not sure," Rosie said, taking the duct tape from her pocket. "I used to think it was a Tasmanian tiger. Now I can't imagine what to call it."

"That fucking thing tried to *kill* me."

"Yes, I know. Please go inside at once. There are two more somewhere on campus."

"Two more? Like *that*?"

Rosie dragged one heavy front paw on top of the other, and pulled out a length of tape. As she began to truss the thylacine, Neil's snotty and nasal breathing triggered her temper.

"For Pete's sake," she yelled. "Hurry. Get indoors while you still can. Move!"

Neil's boots scrambled to gain purchase against the cobblestones, and he ran, footsteps *thud, thud, thudding* into the distance.

9

With only one good hand, Janine had to choose between the leash or the gun. Of course, she chose the gun. No contest. Gingerly, she slipped the handle of the leash over her injured right wrist, dragged it to the crook of her elbow, and closed her arm. She gripped the Smith & Wesson in her left hand. The gun felt strange, unnatural, as if the fingers didn't know what to do. Perhaps they really didn't know, *wouldn't* know, what to do. She swept the thought aside.

"*Ziel*," she said. "*Gehen*." Target. Go.

Zeus took a few paces, stopped, turned to check that everything was okay. The leash must be exerting a different pull on his harness.

"*Gehen*," she urged, and he took off.

They jogged more or less side by side, Zeus slightly in the lead.

Janine glanced at her broken wrist. The skin had turned purple and blue, right down into her palm. And that weird hump… The discolouration and deformity looked nasty, but the break didn't hurt any more. Why not? It seemed ominous. Too much adrenaline in her system? Or nerve damage? For some reason, she was feeling groggy, mentally spaced out. Could she be in shock? Maybe. But she had heard, somewhere, that a broken bone releases marrow into the bloodstream, which causes confusion once the fat globules reach the brain. Shit, was that true? Could she be having a stroke? An old person who breaks a hip is at increased risk of stroke, she knew that for sure. That's what had killed Pa so long ago—

Her phone rang. It was Harvey.

"Two K9 units are heading your way," he said. "ETA fifteen minutes."

Not soon enough. "Okay, thanks for the update."

She hung up, pocketed her phone, and took the gun from her waistband again. Fifteen minutes? She had a feeling this situation would be all over by then. The breeze carried a mizzling rain. Janine gazed up at the clouds. *Hold off*, she thought. *Please, just hold off.*

Zeus, moving towards an orange brick building, came to a stop.

Janine stopped too, and watched him carefully. Had he lost the trail? Was there already too much moisture in the air? She waited for his signal of defeat—sitting down—but instead, he head-checked to the right, lifted his nose high, and sniffed.

Excitement and dread prickled along Janine's spine.

His behaviour meant one thing and one thing only: while following T1's scent trail on the ground, Zeus had picked up T1's fresh scent—and current location—on the wind.

"Good boy," she whispered, almost to herself.

He stood taller, nose higher, ears stiff and forward-facing. Long experience told her that Zeus was double-checking, that she must be patient, not order him to run on. How Zeus could trail a scent, she couldn't even imagine. But it wasn't like following an unravelled ball of string. The process was more dynamic than that. The human nose has six million olfactory receptors compared to a dog's 300 million. Sometimes when they worked together, Janine tried to picture the world as Zeus might see it; not with his eyes, but with his nose, and she always conjured a vista of smoke trails in different colours and hues rising up from every animal, mineral and vegetable on earth, like pin-pricks of steam from a nascent volcano.

Zeus tensed, flicked his ears.

She looked over the Smith & Wesson. Yes, okay to fire.

Zeus head-checked once more, then struck out towards a low-lying building with a peaked tin roof. An abandoned ATV sat half-in-half-out of the building's giant, shattered window. The vehicle's tray held a lawnmower, blower-vac, chainsaw. Janine put the scenario together: one of the groundskeepers, spooked by a tiger, had shat himself and pranged. Nobody was here now. She almost expected tumbleweeds. The sign on the free-standing building read CAMPUS BOOKSHOP. And Zeus was making a beeline for it.

Anxiety dried her mouth.

T1 was inside the bookshop.

No doubt. Because Zeus strained at the leash, trying to run. He only did that when he found the scent-subject and wished to close in for the takedown. The leash handle dug painfully into the crook of Janine's elbow. Closing her arm, hard, she pulled back on the leash. Zeus obeyed and slowed to walking speed. Even so, his muzzle quivered with tension.

"*Vorsichtig, gefahr,*" she said. Careful, danger.

They halted across the road from the bookshop on a grassy median strip. Ice-cold drizzle whirled and swirled on the breeze, cooling Janine's sweating face.

She pointed the gun and observed the shopfront. Closed doors. A floor-to-ceiling window running the length of the building. The ATV had made a hole in the window about three metres by two. Within, the shop held a long, high bookcase, spanning left to right almost wall to wall. Behind would be other bookcases, parallel, in neat rows.

Too many hiding spots.

But T1 was definitely in there.

Janine breathed deeply, once, twice, trying to steady her jitters.

Now what? The other K9 units were about ten minutes away. Should she take the initiative, go inside the shop and hunt the tiger herself, aisle by aisle?

No. Too dangerous.

Okay, she would call Harvey, advise him of her location. Tell him to send in the Special Operations Group. Fully armoured, the SOGgies would storm the bookshop and reduce the tiger to mincemeat with their SIG MCX rifles. Meanwhile, waiting for their arrival, she would stay here on the median strip, *en garde* just in case, her M&P S&W at the ready. She nodded, deliberately exhaled. Having a strategy felt good. She tucked the gun into her waistband, took out her phone, thumbed the touchscreen to scroll for Harvey's number.

And froze.

Oh Christ, that awful *sound*.

A deep, mewling cry with a hoarse, hitching rasp. The tiger, it must be the goddamned tiger. And yes, there it was, standing just inside the shop near the ATV's front bumper, staring at her. With blood over its face. Still wet. Fresh blood. The boy with his ripped throat came to mind. Janine shuddered. Then her joints and muscles locked in fear.

Seconds ticked by.

A stalemate tableau.

Herself, Zeus, and T1, all motionless, all waiting for the other's first move.

Janine slid the phone back into her pocket and closed her quaking fingers around the butt of the gun. *Easy, easy.* No sudden moves. Could she shoot the bastard from this distance? With her left hand? Perhaps she wouldn't have to. Perhaps T1 was simply checking them out, deciding whether or not she and Zeus posed an immediate threat. If they remained still, T1 may well lose interest in such a boring stand-off and turn around, head back into the depths of the bookshop, and please God, that's exactly what would happen, what *will* happen...

With a nimbleness that defied its size, T1 jumped out of the broken window and landed silently, four-footed, on the path. It stopped, still as death, brow furrowed in concentration.

Janine's heart thudded. Zeus strained forward, growling, cutting the lead into the flesh of her arm. The pain cleared her mind. She extended the gun and aimed at the broadest part of T1: its chest. *Never aim for the head*, her instructors at the Academy had always demanded, *it's too small a target*. What if she missed the chest? The gunfire would startle T1, most likely provoke its charge. She couldn't afford to miss. Her finger stuttered on the trigger.

What if she missed?

T1 shifted its weight and reared up on hind legs. Janine felt the blood drain from her face. Oh, *fuck*. The son of a bitch must be over two-metres tall. The gun shook in her hand.

Those eyes.

Those pitch-black eyes.

***

The front legs were already trussed. Rosie panted, sweated, and puffed. The paws were extraordinarily heavy. She wound the duct tape around and around the thylacine's hind legs. A stray tear spilled down her cheek, and she swiped at it impatiently, crossly, with the back of her hand. As soon as Neil the security guard had run off, she had wept and shook for a good half minute. A stress reaction, naturally. Seeing the thylacine attack Neil—*strangle* him, in fact—had been horrific. She would, more than likely, have to endure quite a few nightmares over the upcoming weeks or months. Even years. However, now was not the time to lose courage.

Once the paws were bound, Rosie pushed them off her knees and crawled towards the head of the drugged, snoring creature. T2, according to its ear tag. Blood covered its jaws and snout. Whose blood? Students, lecturers, tutors.

People she knew.

Oh, dear God.

Rosie took a moment to steel herself. Then she pulled out a length of tape, pressed it against the muzzle, and kept wrapping the tape around and around the muzzle until she was satisfied that T2 could not possibly open his mouth—assuming the creature woke up at all. The breathing, though noisy, was irregular and shallow. The tips of sharp, pointed teeth peeked out from under the flews, and the sight made her pause.

Why hadn't T2 bitten Neil? Why attempt to strangle him instead?

It didn't make sense.

Granted, the thylacine's radius and ulna were separate, which allowed rotational wrist movement like that of a cat rather than a dog. The increased wrist flexibility would, theoretically, allow the thylacine more options for subduing quarry. Yet there were no historical records of thylacines exhibiting a chokehold manoeuvre. Kangaroos, on the other hand, commonly included the chokehold in their fighting repertoire. If pursued by a predator—a dingo or wild dog—the kangaroo would try to lead it into a water source, such as a dam, in order to grab the predator by the throat and drown it. But thylacines sharing that particular type of behaviour? At first glance, it didn't seem possible. However, the thylacine and kangaroo shared the same tail configuration. Both animals were marsupials with pouches. So, why not share a fighting technique as well?

Rosie huffed and shook her head.

No, no, *no*, it simply didn't *fit*.

The kangaroo is bipedal, the thylacine a quadruped. More disparities: herbivore versus carnivore; completely different paw configurations; different modes of locomotion. And the thylacine, genetically speaking, was marooned on its own island, with no relatives. Unless…

Rosie considered the red kangaroo "surrogate mothers" that she kept in the enclosure. Not for the first time, she pondered the possibility of genetic corruption of the thylacine litter. Some kind of chemical passed in the milk? Or could it be a hormonal influence from the period of gestation within the Tasmanian devils? Then again, every handling of Tommy, the dead pup in the jar, carried a risk of contamination. Just a single *speck* of human skin could incorporate foreign DNA...

She took off her glasses and rubbed at her eyes.

Bottom line, she had no clue. It is *impossible* to study an animal's natural behaviour when it is kept behind bars. She realised that now. And the realisation hollowed her stomach.

"So, thylacines, huh?" Janine O'Connell, the policewoman, had said.

"Yes. More or less."

"More or less? You've got that right. I saw one of them outside. It was a freak."

Yes, her thylacines were freaks. Rosie had failed. The Thylacine De-Extinction Project was an abject failure, a waste of time, a complete waste of her entire adult life...

Oh, don't be such a baby, she thought, fighting back tears. *You don't have the luxury of indulgence. There are two more thylacines to catch.* The drizzle came down in a brief flurry, slicking the cobblestones. Soaked and freezing, Rosie struggled to her feet. Oh, she ached. She must be covered with bruises.

Then she noticed T2's wound, high on his back leg.

Squatting, she ran both hands through the short, bloodied fur and discovered a hole. Compact, big enough to fit the tip of her finger. A bullet wound from the gun of a police officer. She wondered how O'Connell and her dog might be faring, but such thoughts only skipped her mind straight to Glenn. Please God, let him be all right. And his wife was pregnant again, wasn't she? Children need their father. Glenn's wife, Pam, was far too young to be widowed. Then again, hadn't Rosie been far too young to be widowed? Yet God had showed no mercy in that instance. So, why would He show any mercy now?

Get to work.

The mist became a light and steady rain. A flash of lightning preceded a low rumble of thunder. Rosie picked up the jab stick. Could she remember how to reload it?

Fumbling, she discovered the cocking lever and tried to pull it open. Goodness, it required a lot of muscle power. Gritting her teeth, holding the jab stick tight against her body, straining, she finally managed to cock the lever. Ten ccs. Glenn had told her to draw that much, a deliberate overdose. Rosie felt a stab of regret. Glenn, for all his bogan sensibilities, his exasperating foibles, was a damn good animal handler. Had she ever told him so? She couldn't remember. Probably not. She had never been the type to mollycoddle…

Stop, stop, stop. Concentrate on the task at hand.

Reload the bloody jab stick.

She reached into her top lab pocket and felt something sharp. *Ouch.* Darn it, a vial must have broken. Wrenching out her hand in a sudden panic, Rosie frantically inspected her fingertips for blood. If she had pricked her skin on a glass shard, she might be out like a light within seconds. By the looks of it, however, her skin was intact. She was okay. Was she? Yes. Nevertheless, she held her breath, waiting for any sign of wooziness. Seconds passed.

No, she was absolutely fine.

She must have smashed a vial when T2 had knocked her to the ground. Carefully, she opened her lab pocket and peeked inside. Her heart dropped. All three vials were broken. She had no way to reload the jab stick without returning to the lab.

Defenceless.

It occurred to her in a rush that she had spent the last few minutes lost in thought, with no consideration for her surroundings. What if her thylacines hunted in a pack? She might have been attacked at any moment. Might be attacked at any moment still. Staggered, imagining the pain of teeth sinking into her skull, she gasped, clutched at her throat and stared, wild-eyed, in all directions. Nothing, nobody… she was alone out here, alone and defenceless in the yellowed, darkening gloom of a brewing thunderstorm.

Damn, damn, damn, damn, *damn*.

She would take the jab stick with her anyway. If nothing else, she could use it as a club.

Hurrying down the laneway and past the dumpsters, she tried the nearest door. Locked. Probably *all* the rear doors to the cafés would be locked. Panic made her hyperventilate. What should she do? Return to the lab? Oh, but it was such a long walk across campus, and with no weapon... No, she would head into the food court plaza, find a restaurant with an open door, hole up inside, and wait for the authorities to deliver her.

She had decommissioned one thylacine. That was enough for now.

***

Framed by the broken window of the bookshop, reared up on hind legs, forepaws held straight out and hanging at the wrists, T1 resembled a kangaroo but one from a dark and twisted hallucination. Yet the monster appeared calm, chest muscles loose, brow smooth.

Was T1 curious? Angry? Fearful? Cautious?

Despite Janine's know-how in deciphering canine body language, she felt at a loss. Maybe the moniker "Tasmanian tiger" was accurate. Maybe this animal behaved more like a cat than a dog. Janine had zero experience with cats, spurning them as aloof, snippy, temperamental animals. What might a cat lover make of T1's behaviour?

Okay, regardless, Janine must search for micro-signs.

Direct eye contact flagged imminent attack in most animal species, humans included, but she couldn't tell for sure if T1 was even looking at her. Its eyeballs were completely black. No "whites," no colour differentiation, nothing to suggest an iris.

An animal that has a tail might hold it stiff and upright when feeling threatened or aggressive. The tiger's tail rested on the ground as a stabiliser. No clue there, either.

No growling, no teeth-baring, the ears relaxed.

Shit.

Could she and Zeus back off? Or were they already embroiled in a fight? Either way, Janine had a duty, and that was to kill this son of a bitch before it could hurt anybody else.

As if reading her mind, T1 lowered its massive head and raised its hackles. The cropped fur lifted in rows like a flowering pine cone, one row after another. The weird sight tightened Janine's gut. T1 dropped its jaw, wide, ever so wide, to reveal long teeth, a red tongue, corrugated hard palate, dark maw beyond. The drawn-out hiss sounded reptilian.

Holy fucking *Christ.*

Janine tried to swallow.

Zeus pulled at the leash.

"All right," she whispered, finger tightening on the trigger. "Here goes nothing."

Janine straightened her arm, willing away the shakes, and pulled the trigger.

Crack.

The tiger bounded, yelped. Blood erupted from its shoulder.

A hit, a direct hit!

Janine felt a wild and crazy elation. She fired again. Missed. A piece of the bookshop's unbroken window exploded and rained down on the ATV's crumpled bonnet.

Zeus lunged forward, wrenching the leash and unbalancing her. Janine fell, sprawling onto the median strip, the handle of the leash ripping over her broken wrist as Zeus bolted free. The explosion of pain took her breath, tunnelled her vision.

"*Komm zuruk*," she gasped. Come back.

Growling, hissing, awful howls—ghoulish sounds—demonic shrieks from Hell.

Janine struggled to her knees. She groped for the dropped gun. Zeus, his muzzle pulled back into a snarl, leapt about, snapping. The tiger was unfazed. More than double Zeus's size, T1 swung its head, watchful, as if waiting for the right opportunity to attack. It would be an uneven fight. Within the next few moments, Zeus would lose the fight, and his life.

"*Komm zuruk*," Janine yelled.

The two animals charged and clashed.

T1's jaws closed about Zeus's ear and sheared it from his scalp. Janine stumbled to her feet and ran, gun outstretched, screaming in desperation, anger, terror. Zeus and T1 were locked within an insane and frenetic dance, shifting, turning, whirling, barking, gnashing. If she pulled the trigger at the wrong split-second, she would shoot Zeus. But if she hesitated, held out for the perfect shot, Zeus would be dead anyway.

They had been partners for six years. She had never had a better colleague, a better friend, a loyal spirit she trusted more. They ate breakfast together every morning, often fell asleep on the couch together watching TV after a long shift, his head resting on her lap.

Fuck it.

Janine shouldered into the brawl and closed the bruised, nerve-deadened fingers of her right hand around T1's front paw.

Her cheek opened under its teeth. Another bite, and the side of Zeus's face turned into a shower of blood, his caramel eyes staring wide enough to show the vein-threaded whites.

Janine rammed the gun hard up into the tiger's armpit and pulled the trigger.

The bulk of the animal's body muffled the sound of gunfire. Hot gases blasted Janine's hand like a million little needles. T1 jerked and grunted, coughed, releasing from its mouth a fine spray of blood. *Lung shot.*

She pulled the trigger again, over and over.

Tottering, black eyeballs staring straight at her, the tiger reeled on its back feet, tongue lolling and lashing, blood gargling and choking in its throat. As T1 fell, Janine followed it to the ground, holding tight to its paw, her broken wrist ringing with pain. She dropped both knees into the bastard's ribs and punched the barrel of the gun under its jaw.

One final connection, eye to eye, the monster hacking and gasping.

Bang.

Brains erupted out of its head in a vomit of red curds.

The tiger slumped, lifeless.

Losing her balance, Janine fell across T1. Breathless, she couldn't move. Its fur scraped against her flesh, short and stiff as a nailbrush. She would never forget that sensation for as long as she lived. The agony in her wrist threatened to make her faint. With effort, she rolled away and collapsed, supine, on the road. The rain pelted softly, a gentle and cool welcome. Consciousness winked away.

Snuffling, whimpering sounds...

Janine's eyelids flickered. Zeus, brows knitted with concern, was licking at her face.

"Hey," she whispered, and her tongue felt thick and swollen in her mouth. "Hey, we did it. We fucking did it."

Zeus's right ear hung from his head in a grisly, steaming fold. Fuck. She must help him, try to staunch the bleeding. Janine sat up. Hot liquid ran down her neck. What the hell? Could it be rain? Hot rain in winter? She felt along her face with her good hand, and found the gory skin flap. Blood pumped over her fingertips. The cheek, peeled away, dangled past her jawline. The exposed flesh had the soft give of a raw eye-fillet steak.

Nausea rose the bile to the back of her throat.

How deep the injury, she had no idea. Superficial and skin only? Or was the whole side of her face sheared down to the bone? Would ruined facial muscles give her a permanent droop, a kind of palsy? She didn't know. Her eyes rolled in their sockets. The dark, writhing clouds wheeled in ever-tightening circles. *No*, Janine thought. *Don't pass out again.*

She smoothed the skin flap up and over her face. With the back of her numb and injured hand, she did the same to Zeus, pressing his ruined flesh tight against his skull. They would have matching scars. In the distance, sirens sounded. Their fight was over. Thank Christ.

"We're going to be all right," she slurred. "Good boy. You're such a good boy."

Zeus buried his nose, cold and wet, into her neck. She managed a smile, but with only one side of her mouth.

"Oh, yes," she muttered, as the sirens got louder, closer. "You're my good boy."

10

Rosie held the jab stick on one shoulder and strode out from the laneway.

The food court plaza was a group of buildings arranged in a square, with all four "corners" missing to allow egress. In the centre sat a gravelled section, with a metal statue of an emu that had always struck her as looking faintly ridiculous.

The rain poured down harder. Rosie's spectacles became dotted and steamy, but she couldn't take them off. Without them, she was as blind as the proverbial bat.

Sirens. About time. Hopefully, the campus was filling with police cars and ambulances.

The closest restaurant happened to be the Romaine Salad Bar. It offered a terrific Chicken Caesar. She tried the door. Locked. Blast it. Scurrying, she headed to the next when something awful caught the tail of her eye and she froze. Dread moved through her in a long, shuddering wave. For a moment, she couldn't turn her head, couldn't bear to look. Her heart boomed and blatted against her ribs.

She looked. And dry heaved.

Yes, it was a leg.

A lower leg, severed at the knee. Lying on the pavement directly outside the Cravetarian restaurant, the stump resting in a puddle of blood. A bare leg. A man's leg, hairy and stocky. Wearing a thick woollen sock, and a brown leather pull-on work boot.

She lifted a clawed hand to her throat, scrabbling for the gold cross on a chain that had not hung about her neck for decades.

Instead, she clutched at the lapels of her lab coat and pulled them tightly together.

Glenn.

Dear God. That was *Glenn's* leg.

She tried to catch her breath. The jab stick slipped out of her other hand and fell to the ground. Clenching her teeth, she made her way over, creeping, one cautious step after the other. Perhaps Glenn was nearby, terribly injured but alive. That was possible, wasn't it? A severed leg didn't automatically mean death. He could be hiding inside Cravetarian, a make-do tourniquet ratcheted tightly around his thigh.

"Glenn?" she said, her voice too hoarse to carry.

Slowly now, terrified, advancing in a wide circle as if the leg could animate and attack, Rosie approached. The tibia and fibula bones, unnaturally twined together, jutted from the ripped meat of the joint. It seemed as if the lower leg had been *twisted* off, as one would twist the drumstick of a roasted chicken. She pressed both sets of knuckles to her mouth and let out a stifled cry of horror. *Buck up*, she ordered herself. Quit simpering. A member of staff was hurt and needed urgent help.

"Glenn?" she said again, her voice a little stronger. "Where are you?"

Her gaze hunted the ground nearby.

Spotted the blood trail.

A long swipe of gore led to the open door of Cravetarian. So, the attack had happened inside that restaurant. The thylacine had dragged Glenn's leg out into the rain. She faced the doorway. Her muscles locked and shivered. Her feet had become too heavy to lift.

"Are you in there? Can you hear me?"

Squeezing her hands into fists, she lifted her trembling chin and walked to the door. Scattered tables and chairs, smashed plates of food, more blood. She gripped the door frame, fighting off a wave off dizziness. She stepped inside. Had to cover her nose. Good Lord, the air smelled *terrible*. The hot coppery stink of blood, the odour of shit.

Nearby lay Glenn's jab stick. Faltering, having to lean against the wall to maintain balance, she squatted and picked it up. The safety cuff was off. The syringe held ten ccs of tranquilliser. Whatever had happened in this place had happened *fast*. No time for Glenn to defend himself. And he was damn quick with a jab stick too. Many times, she had watched him use the device in the animal enclosure, and had admired his dexterity and speed. (But had she ever told him of her admiration? She couldn't recall.)

"Glenn?" she said. "Can you hear me?"

There.

There by the counter.

She felt herself blanch. Another leg. A whole one, torn off at the hip. What about the rest of him? Where was he? *Where was he?* Stumbling beyond upended tables, shoving aside chairs, Rosie hastened past the counter. The crepe soles of her flats squeaked and lost purchase in a lake of blood. She nearly fell. Caught herself against a table. Blinked, kept blinking.

Tried to make sense of the scene.

Couldn't *comprehend* the scene.

An explosion of blood over the floor, furniture, high ceiling. Coils of loosely strewed intestines. A liver, a ruptured kidney. Entrails still warm and steaming. A headless torso leaning against the wall, as if propped there on purpose like a store mannequin, the shredded khaki shirt soaked in gore, the abdominal cavity split apart. Further, towards the back wall, an arm here, another arm there. By the toilet door, lying on its ear, facing away from her, Glenn's head, the long hair sodden with sticky, drying clots.

The thylacines must have attacked him en masse, and pulled him apart.

Drawn and quartered him.

Of their own volition, Rosie's feet began stepping backwards. The need to scream felt like a hard boulder in the pit of her stomach. The boulder was rising, rising. She crashed into furniture, her feet still hurrying backwards. Her throat swelled and gagged on the upcoming scream. She staggered outside. The rain pelted her in driving sheets. She couldn't breathe. Couldn't draw a single breath.

Then the scream tore its way out.

Her lungs sucked in a huge draught of air and she screamed again and again, madly, hysterically, as if she would never be able to stop.

Yip, yip, yip.

She spun around. Standing by the emu statue in the middle of the square was a thylacine.

The sight brought her to her senses. Now, she understood. Oh, this meeting was no coincidence. Finding two thylacines on a campus of this size, by sheer luck? Of course not. The remaining members of the pack had been following her all along, stalking her, as they must have been following and stalking Glenn.

And directly, she would receive the exact same treatment as they had given him.

***

The scream jolted Janine, waking her as if from a dream. Zeus's one good ear pricked. Two more desperate screams, in quick succession, from somewhere nearby, somewhere close behind them. Then nothing. Jesus fucking *Christ*.

Janine struggled to her feet. Letting go of her face allowed the flap of torn cheek to droop and slap wetly against her jaw. Stars momentarily blinded her as her vision dimmed. She picked up the gun. Panting, hobbling, weaving from side to side, she moved away from the bookshop towards a long, single-storey building perhaps fifty metres distant. She could barely make it out in the heavy rain. A mist was rolling down from the Yarra Ranges in a series of ragged, unfurling flags, spreading out. Soon, the campus would be engulfed.

Janine's feet, long used to jogging, found a rhythm at last, and she sped up.

Zeus stayed by her side. Damn, she felt proud.

"We're a great team," she said thickly, and spat, her mouth full of blood.

A sign up ahead: FOOD COURT PLAZA.

The building must be a terrace of restaurants. Just visible were the identical back doors, the identical high windows, each feature regularly spaced along the brick wall.

How many bullets did she have left? No clue. Maybe five? Her right hand didn't work anymore; the wrist had swollen grotesquely, must be compressing nerves and tendons. If she ejected the magazine to check, she might not be able to push it back in again single-handed. Besides, she had already swapped out one magazine for the only spare.

The rain hitting the exposed flesh of her cheek began to sting. *Uh oh, here comes the pain*, she thought grimly. No doubt it would hurt like a bitch.

***

The rain came down. Rosie and the thylacine stared at each other, neither of them moving. A strange, nihilistic calm descended upon Rosie, washing away the panic and fear. Perhaps looking through the wet, foggy lenses of her spectacles had provoked a dissociative state, similar to the detachment achieved when, say, a war photographer looks through the camera and forgets that he or she is physically present at the scene. Or perhaps—more likely—the scales had at last fallen from Rosie's eyes.

"Not my Adam," she murmured, "but my Lucifer."

Could she duck into Cravetarian with enough time to shut the door behind her? Perhaps. But hiding behind a closed door was simply out of the question now.

The thylacine bared its teeth.

Rosie smiled back, in kind, a tight-lipped grimace.

There was only one course of action. She had brought this monstrosity into the world, which meant she had a responsibility to destroy it—or at least to *try* and destroy it. No matter what the consequence. Lifting her chin, she took the jab stick in both hands, and plodded onto the gravelled centre square.

The thylacine tensed, leg muscles flexing, head lowering.

"I am not asking, Lord, that you take this trial away," Rosie said gently. "Instead, I simply ask that Your will be done in my life. Whatever that means, that is what I want."

Glory be, she hadn't said that prayer in a long, long time. Not since that last day at the hospital, when she had held her husband's hand, and wept. God had decided, in His infinite wisdom, moving as He did in His mysterious way, to allow Vin to die from the heart attack. Vin, who had never smoked a single cigarette in his life. Who had kept fit and trim with golf, with rambling walks after dinner alongside Rosie when they would talk about this and that, mostly subjects concerning science, since Vin had been a scientist too, a professor of theoretical physics. And, oh yes, a non-drinker. Vincent Giuliani, love of her life, dead at thirty-four.

She smoothed her wet hair back from her face, kept steadily walking onwards.

How did the rest of the prayer go? She couldn't remember the next few lines. And then—

Please, Lord, give me the strength that I need to face today. I don't have to worry about tomorrow. If you just give me the strength that I need today that is all I need. Keep me from sinning during this trial. Instead, help me to keep my eyes on you. You are the Holy Lord, and all of my hope rests in you…

Hah. No use praying. Religion had failed her.

Science had failed her.

What was left?

Nothing. A meaningless, random, chaotic vacuum of nothing.

Growling, the thylacine dropped open its lower jaw. Rosie was close enough to see the coloured ear tag: T4. The thylacine that Glenn liked to call Boomer. Oh, Glenn had thought his pet names for the animals were private, his own little secret, but over the years, he had slipped now and then. Why, just this morning, before Bill De Vries and Simon had arrived, Glenn had referred to K2 as Mabel. Rosie had always admired Glenn's devotion to his animal charges. How despicable that the thylacines hadn't felt the same admiration. Rosie frowned, gritted her jaw. Why tear Glenn apart, rend him limb from limb? Why? *Why?*

"Why?" she screamed.

The creature hissed, raised its hackles.

Perhaps ten metres lay between them.

"What was your part in the killing, I wonder?" she said, her voice steady and clear. "Did you rip off his arms or legs? Take out his innards? Decapitate him? Good gracious, how could you have hated him so much? You wretched beast. Didn't he care for you every single day of your miserable, godforsaken life?"

Distracted, the thylacine turned its head.

Rosie stiffened, abruptly halted. *My end has come,* she thought, heart thudding. Here is another thylacine. Together they will shred me to pieces.

"Look out!" a garbled voice yelled.

Jogging towards her, good God, was the policewoman, Janine O'Connell, so badly mauled and covered in blood, it was a miracle she could stay on her feet. And the dog, Zeus, for pity's sake, with half its face hanging off. O'Connell raised a gun, arm shaking. And she *kept on running*. Straight towards the thylacine. As if she meant to go right up to the blasted thing and push the gun barrel flush against its temple.

"Stay back from it!" Rosie shrieked. "Stay back!"

The gun fired. The report echoed off the shopfronts. Startled but clearly unhurt, T4 baulked, turned, and loped away.

"Fuck," O'Connell said, and spat out a long rope of blood.

She didn't slow down, nor did the dog. They hurried across the gravel in pursuit. Neither of them gave Rosie a single glance. T4 left the plaza, striking out in the direction of the student administration building. The gun went off again, to no apparent effect. Another miss?

"Wait for me," Rosie shouted, and broke into a run.

Lightning blazed. Thunder crashed directly overhead. The rain intensified, so loud it hurt the ears, a yammering, concussive hiss striking every surface. A smoke-grey fog tumbled down from the hills beyond, pushing across the campus. The last few buildings in the distance faded, became milky silhouettes, as the fog engulfed them.

Ahead, T4 had picked up to a trot. O'Connell and Zeus were running after it, hell for leather, too fast for Rosie.

"Stop," she called, breathless. "It's a trap."

Hopeless. Her voice couldn't possibly carry over this downpour, this driving wind.

But it *was* a trap, she was sure of it. An ambush, like what must have happened to Glenn. The creature was leading them to the surviving members of the pack. But how many could be left out of the six? Rosie scrambled to think.

T6 dead in its cage along with the activist girl. *One.*

T3 and T5 dead in the main lab. *That's three.*

T2 drugged and trussed like a turkey by Rosie's own hand. *That's four.*

So, only T4 and T1 left—unless O'Connell and Zeus had already dispatched T1. They had been tracking it, after all. How else could they have sustained such appalling injuries? Perhaps only T4 remained. A single thylacine against a loaded jab stick and loaded pistol? Oh, she liked those odds. Liked them an awful lot.

Another gunshot.

She flicked a finger to clear the lenses of her spectacles. Wait, O'Connell seemed to be listing to one side. Or was that a trick of the atmosphere? *Confound this fog*, Rosie thought. The descending mist had all but obscured the blue-green canopy of the nearby hillside.

Hillside?

Rosie gasped. Oh, why hadn't she realised this earlier? The Yarra Ranges, the Alpine National Park, the Kosciuszko National Park. Thousands and thousands of hectares of open forest. If T4 fled into that wilderness, the creature would be gone for good. And in the surrounds of those parks were so many rural communities, farmlands, so many people...

Despite the lancing stitch in her side, Rosie pushed herself to run faster. She *must* catch up. The pain in her shoulder and arm muscles flamed white-hot with the weight of the jab stick. Buildings, signs, abandoned cars, bollards, median strips, everything kept appearing suddenly, like a jump scare, out of the fog. She could only just make out the navy blur of O'Connell's uniform, getting fainter and fainter.

"Wait," she panted, "wait."

And there, becoming visible up ahead, the roof of the biochemistry department.

Situated at the northern side of Fraser University, the biochemistry department butted up against the back fence. Well, *fence* was hardly the word; the simple structure, less than a metre high, comprised metal stakes spaced wide apart with two rows of wire strung between them. T4 would be able to leap over it without effort—

Had O'Connell stopped running?

Yes, yes, Rosie was closing in, and quickly. O'Connell appeared to be hunched over. Zeus materialised through the fog and rain, standing next to O'Connell.

In another few metres, Rosie joined them.

Her lungs were on fire. She coughed and spluttered. After a few seconds, when she had recovered somewhat, she regarded O'Connell. The policewoman, shoulders slumped, looked like death itself. The uninjured side of her face shone a sickly, jaundiced yellow. How much blood had the woman lost? Too much and with no sign of slowing. Despite the volume of rainfall, O'Connell stood in a sustained red-tinged puddle. Good *God.* And her right arm. The deformed wrist and bruised hand were a single, swollen mass, tight and round as a football.

"You need to hide and rest," Rosie said. "Immediately."

"No, I don't."

"Try the door of that building over there. I'll make sure an ambulance comes for you."

"Shut up." Drooling bloody spittle, O'Connell pointed the gun dead ahead, shaking it for emphasis.

Rosie looked.

T4 stood by the fence. Wisps of fog curled and rolled about its long, wolfish legs. The creature was staring at them, completely motionless, as still as a post, in that unnatural manner which had always raised the hairs on the back of Rosie's neck. A warm-blooded animal somehow holding itself as rigid as a reptile. How? She had never been able to reconcile this abnormal behaviour. This, more than anything, showed that she had failed to resurrect a genuine thylacine. She could see the truth now, the whole dismal truth.

Damn this abomination.

"Can you shoot it from here?" she said.

"Fuck knows. I've missed every shot so far."

"How many shots do you have left?"

O'Connell shrugged, never taking her eyes off the thylacine.

Sirens keened. The sounds ebbed and flowed on the wind. It was impossible to tell whether or not the emergency vehicles were getting closer. Rosie hoisted the jab stick.

"Hide inside the building and take your dog," she said. "I'll sedate the tiger."

"How? By using that fucking thing like a bayonet?" O'Connell dropped her head, opened her mouth, and let out a long slaver of blood. "No. Don't go near that son of a bitch."

Zeus whined and fidgeted, as if eager to charge.

"*Warten*," O'Connell said.

The dog sat and shifted about on its haunches.

Rosie said, "I'll be careful. If I approach slowly, it might remain still long enough for me to give the injection."

"If you approach, slow or not, that bastard will take your fucking head off."

"Then so be it."

Rosie shouldered the jab stick. She had taken only two steps when the gun fired, deafening her. T4 did not react. Flustered, Rosie looked back, incredulous.

O'Connell spat again. "Fuck. I'm seeing double. That's the problem."

"Do you want me to have a go?"

"You ever shot a gun before?"

"No, I'm afraid not."

O'Connell straightened and began to stagger towards T4, gun held at a faltering arm's length. Zeus followed on one side of her. Rosie hurried to keep up on the other. Still, the creature didn't move.

Six metres and closing.

Rosie wielded the jab stick in both hands. Zeus began to growl.

T4 rocked back and raised itself on hind legs, balancing with its tail, rearing high into the air, looking and behaving like nothing alive on this earth, jaws agape, a kind of prehistoric brute from the Megafauna age.

Three metres and closing.

Rosie felt a tremulous, awful desperation, a giddy sensation of standing at the abyss with no way back. The creature hunkered, tensing every muscle, readying to spring. And when it did, Rosie would punch the bloody jab stick right into its black heart.

The creature sprang.

But not towards them. With a sideways flick of its back legs, in a manner reminiscent of a kicking goat kid, it launched itself up and over the fence. Landing on all fours, it began to crash away through the undergrowth.

"No!" Rosie wailed.

O'Connell fired. The gun clicked and nothing happened. Empty. She let out a long, tired moan and let the gun slip through her fingers and drop to the ground. The jab stick, as if it had a mind of its own, somehow fell from Rosie's grasp too.

T4 bolted up the hillside, zigzagging between trees, its passage flagged by the whipping and snapping of ferns and shrubs, the occasional flourish of its tail. Rosie strained her eyes to follow. And then the creature was gone. Now, only the forest and creeping fog remained, the glare of lightning, boom of thunder.

Rosie's knees felt weak. She locked them in order to stay upright. Her chin trembled. The rain teemed down. Her glasses fogged.

"Will it survive?" O'Connell said thickly.

Rosie considered. Before today, she would have said, *No, absolutely not.* T4, like his brothers, had lived its entire life inside a cage with no mother to teach it how to hunt, find water, shelter.

But after witnessing their cunning? Sheer brutality? Intelligence? ESP?

A single siren approached from behind, loud and piercing, and cut out. The sound of a running motor. Wearily, Rosie glanced over her shoulder. A police car. Thank God. O'Connell would get help. And by the looks of her poor, ravaged face, she would need all the help she could get under heaven. Car doors opened and slammed. Uniformed figures moved towards them through a blaze of headlights.

"Hey, answer me," O'Connell said. "Will the bastard survive out there or not?"

A cloud squatted over the hills, obscuring the forest behind a gauzy veil.

"I don't know," Rosie said, tears rising. "I honestly haven't the faintest notion."

Then strong hands were gripping her arms. She felt her knees give out. A policeman was speaking to her, but Rosie couldn't make out any words. He carried her in his arms to the car.

END

ABOUT THE AUTHOR

Deborah Sheldon is a professional writer from Melbourne, Australia. Latest releases, all traditionally published, include the horror collection *Perfect Little Stitches and Other Stories*, the horror novel *Devil Dragon*, and the romance-suspense novella *The Long Shot*.

Her short fiction has appeared in many well-respected magazines such as Aurealis, SQ Mag, Midnight Echo, Island, and Quadrant, as well as in numerous anthologies. Her work has been shortlisted for various Australian Shadows Awards. Other credits include TV scripts, feature articles, non-fiction books (Reed Books, Random House Australia), and award-winning medical writing. Visit Deb at http://deborahsheldon.wordpress.com

SEVERED**PRESS**

 facebook.com/severedpress
 twitter.com/severedpress

CHECK OUT OTHER GREAT HORROR NOVELS

BLACK FRIDAY
by Michael Hodges

Jared the kleptomaniac, Chike the unemployed IT guy, Patricia the shopaholic, and Jeff the meth dealer are trapped inside a Chicago supermall on Black Friday. Bridgefield Mall empties during a fire alarm, and most of the shoppers drive off into a strange mist surrounding the mall parking lot. They never return. Chike and his group try calling friends and family, but their smart phones won't work, not even Twitter. As the mist creeps closer, the mall lights flicker and surge. Bulbs shatter and spray glass into the air. Unsettling noises are heard from within the mist, as the meth dealer becomes unhinged and hunts the group within the mall. Cornered by the mist, and hunted from within, Chike and the survivors must fight for their lives while solving the mystery of what happened to Bridgefield Mall. Sometimes, a good sale just isn't worth it.

GRIMWEAVE
by Tim Curran

In the deepest, darkest jungles of Indochina, an ancient evil is waiting in a forgotten, primeval valley. It is patient, monstrous, and bloodthirsty. Perfectly adapted to its hot, steaming environment, it strikes silent and stealthy, it chosen prey: human. Now Michael Spiers, a Marine sniper, the only survivor of a previous encounter with the beast, is going after it again. Against his better judgement, he is made part of a Marine Force Recon team that will hunt it down and destroy it.

The hunters are about to become the hunted.

CHECK OUT OTHER GREAT HORROR NOVELS

DEATH CRAWLERS
by Gerry Griffiths

Worldwide, there are thought to be 8,000 species of centipede, of which, only 3,000 have been scientifically recorded. The venom of Scolopendra gigantea—the largest of the arthropod genus found in the Amazon rainforest—is so potent that it is fatal to small animals and toxic to humans. But when a cargo plane departs the Amazon region and crashes inside a national park in the United States, much larger and deadlier creatures escape the wreckage to roam wild, reproducing at an astounding rate. Entomologist, Frank Travis solicits small town sheriff Wanda Rafferty's help and together they investigate the crash site. But as a rash of gruesome deaths befalls the townsfolk of Prospect, Frank and Wanda will soon discover how vicious and cunning these new breed of predators can be. Meanwhile, Jake and Nora Carver, and another backpacking couple, are venturing up into the mountainous terrain of the park. If only they knew their fun-filled weekend is about to become a living nightmare.

THE PULLER
by Michael Hodges

Matt Kearns has two choices: fight or hide. The creature in the orchard took the rest. Three days ago, he arrived at his favorite place in the world, a remote shack in Michigan's Upper Peninsula. The plan was to mourn his father's death and figure out his life. Now he's fighting for it. An invisible creature has him trapped. Every time Matt tries to flee, he's dragged backwards by an unseen force. Alone and with no hope of rescue, Matt must escape the Puller's reach. But how do you free yourself from something you cannot see?

www.ingramcontent.com/pod-product-compliance
Lightning Source LLC
Chambersburg PA
CBHW061249170626
46809CB00007B/2910